David S. Williams

Give Me Back
My Pride

A Pan Original

First published 1985 by Pan Books Ltd,
Cavaye Place, London SW10 9PG
9 8 7 6 5 4 3 2
(c) David S. Williams 1985
ISBN 0 330 2838 2

Printed and bound in Great Britain by
Hunt Barnard Printing, Aylesbury, Bucks

Chapter 1

As soon as the front door bell rang, my heart gave a jump and started beating faster; my legs went as weak as jelly and I had to gulp hard to control the churning in my stomach. I didn't have to be told who it was. It was David Lucas, one of the sixth formers at the local comprehensive school, come to take me to the barbecue on the beach. My first date – my very first – and as I looked at myself in my dressing-table mirror, I prayed with all my heart that it wouldn't be the last.

Seconds later, my mother shouted up from the foot of the stairs. 'Dianne! It's David . . .' I think she was almost as excited as I was. 'He's just arrived.'

As I made a last-minute check in the mirror, smoothing down the brilliant white t-shirt I'd bought that afternoon, I knew that it had been worth it – even though it had taken my last penny. It showed off my figure to perfection and my freshly washed hair, bleached slightly by a colour tint, looked better than it had for ages. I paused for a second at the top of the stairs and, taking a deep breath, walked down to the living room with far more composure than I felt inside.

David was perched on the edge of one of the large thickly upholstered armchairs, talking to my father. He was tall – an inch over six foot – with fair wavy hair that flopped untidily over a broad forehead. He looked up as I walked in, his light blue eyes glancing up and down, making my stomach flutter wildly.

Then he smiled. 'Hi!' he said, his nervousness betrayed by a slight tremor in his voice. 'I'm sorry if I'm early.'

I smiled back at him. 'It's all right,' I replied with ridiculous bashfulness for a sixteen-year-old. 'I was almost ready anyway.'

There was a moment's silence, an awkward pause, as I struggled to find something to say. Then my mother called from the kitchen, unwittingly saving me from an absurd situation.

'Dianne! Come and give me a hand with the coffees, please!'

She was smiling as I walked in, and she raised her eyebrows in approval. 'He's nice,' she whispered. 'If I were your age, I think I'd fancy him myself . . .'

Afraid that he could hear, I shook my head and my eyes flashed an embarrassed warning. Even so, I felt a flush of pleasure flood through me. I'd been keen on David Lucas for months – ever since the first Upper School disco which the sixth form had organised – but though he'd often spoken to me as we walked down the hill to the large comprehensive school which served our small seaside town, I'd long given up any hope that he'd ask me out.

Then, only the previous evening, as we were strolling home from the youth club with Erica and Bob, he'd asked me if I'd like to come to the barbecue some of his friends were organising.

I was so surprised that all I could do was stammer a reply.

'Great!' His eyes were shining with pleasure as though he'd had some doubts that I'd accept. 'I'll pick you up at half-past seven.'

I walked into the house in a daze. He'd asked me out! When I'd least expected it, he'd actually asked me out! I just couldn't believe it, and afterwards as I lay in bed listening to the distant chimes of a church clock, I had to keep on telling myself that David Lucas had asked me out at last. It really was true.

But then I realised I had nothing new to wear — except for a pair of jeans I'd bought a week earlier and had hardly worn.

So that morning I was in a frenzy of indecision, wondering what to wear. Nothing seemed good enough and I spent most of the day scouring the town for a top to go with my jeans, my despair growing as I wandered from shop to shop without finding anything suitable. I was about to give up when I stopped outside an expensive boutique in a side street, and there in the window was exactly what I'd been looking for: a white dolman-sleeved top in soft single jersey cotton with a V back.

But the price on the ticket made me gasp. It was much more than I'd intended paying, but counting my money and finding that I had just enough, I walked in boldly and bought it. I didn't regret it. I'd seen the look of approval in David's eyes and that was good enough for me.

When I returned to the living room with the tray, he and Dad were talking about football as though they had known each other for years. Mum poured the coffee and as we all sat talking, I became increasingly aware that they liked him.

David glanced at his watch. 'We'd better go,' he said. 'The bus leaves at eight.'

So, hooking a duffel bag containing my towels over my shoulder and clutching in my right hand a cool-bag which Mum had packed with food, we hurried down the road to the bus stop. Mum and Dad had come to the door with us and waved goodbye. And as we got on to the bus, I could still remember Dad's indulgent smile and the silent caution in Mum's eyes as, flushed and excited, I'd kissed her goodbye.

The barbecue was being held about a hundred yards from the end of the promenade, in a large hollow which over the years the wind had scooped out of the sand dunes. The sun was low in the sky when we arrived and most of the others were there before us; in the gathering dusk, we could see their shapes outlined against a large flickering fire. As we trudged towards them, our feet sinking into the cool sand, Bob came to greet us.

'You're just in time,' he yelled above the blare of pop music from a transistor radio. 'We're just about to go for a dip.'

Tall and angular, with auburn hair burnished in tight waves in the fading light of the setting sun, he was already in his swimming trunks. Erica had changed too, though she had a blue wrap skirt with red, green and yellow spots over a matching one-piece swim suit.

'Give them a chance,' she said, helping me unpack my cool-bag. 'Let them put their potatoes in the fire first, or they'll never get cooked in time.'

While David changed a few yards away, we put the foil-wrapped potatoes in the hot ashes on the fringes of the fire.

'Thought you weren't coming,' she said. 'Thought you might have changed your mind.'

She was my closest friend – had been since we started primary school together – and we were about the same height. But while my hair was normally a

fairish brown, she had a halo of short dark hair sur-
rounding a pretty elfin face with a matching mis-
chievous smile. She was, I knew, deliberately goading
me.

'If you think that, you must be crazy,' I replied,
making sure first that David couldn't hear.

We had very few secrets from each other and she
knew I'd been longing for a chance like this for months
– and I told her so.

'Looks like you're leaving nothing to chance tonight
though,' she commented, glancing at my new top.

Her words made my stomach go into tight little
knots, but before I could reply, David called out.

'I'm ready when you are.'

Though he had fair hair, his slim muscular body had
a healthy glowing tan from long days spent under the
hot August sun. Just looking at him made my heart
beat faster.

'Won't be a minute,' I replied.

Fortunately, I'd already changed into my bikini at
home, so all I had to do was slip out of my jeans and
top. Then, taking the hand he offered me, we ran
together to the breakers that were pounding on to the
shore just fifty yards away. Then my toes were digging
into wet sand and as we splashed into the rippling tide,
David shook his hand free. He threw himself forward,
plunging head-first into a curling wave and disappeared under a thrashing torrent of foam. A second
later, I hurled myself after him and felt the water close
over my head.

I surfaced a few feet away from him, surprised that
the sea was so warm.

'It's great, isn't it?' he yelled, spluttering as another
wave crashed against his back.

Shaking the water from my eyes, I had to agree. But then, even if it had been icy cold, it would have been great just to have been with him.

We spent almost half an hour in the sea, our shrieks ringing out in the still night air as we splashed about. Someone brought down a large multi-coloured ball which we played a primitive kind of game with, girls against boys, and we girls gave them a good run for their money. Which wasn't surprising, considering that many of us were in the school netball team. But as the sun, a huge crimson ball in the western sky, began to sink slowly into the burning waters of the bay, it began to get cold. As though at a given signal, we hurried back up the beach and sat huddled around the fire, thick towels wrapped round our shivering shoulders.

Someone had put on more driftwood and had erected over the fire a large metal grid on which we placed the beefburgers and sausages. Mum had buttered hunks of crusty French bread and filled them with salad – enough to feed an army as it happened – which was just as well, seeing that the sea had given us all a ravenous appetite. For about a quarter of an hour, we all munched our food, too hungry to talk even.

Then later, as we sat around the glowing embers of the fire, one of the members of the school orchestra began playing ballads on his guitar and we all sang. There was a kind of magic in the air that night, and when David put his arm around my shoulder and smiled at me, his strong even teeth gleaming in the semi-darkness, my heart almost burst with happiness.

All too soon, it was time to catch the last bus home, and as we trudged back to the coach station, I felt trepidation grow inside me, ousting the bubbling joy and replacing it with a sick apprehension.

What if he didn't ask me out again?

We left Erica and Bob at the corner of our street and David walked me to the door. Both of us were strangely silent as we stood under the porch.

'Thanks for a fantastic evening,' he said, his voice strangely formal. 'And thank your mother too . . . for all the food she made us.'

I looked down at the ground, my eyes beginning to mist over. This was it, I thought: thanks and goodbye.

But then he went on. 'You wouldn't like to come over to my place tomorrow, would you?' When I couldn't reply, he went on hastily, mistaking my inability to speak for reluctance. 'We could ask Bob and Erica over . . . play some records . . .'

I gulped and looked up. 'Oh, David. I'd love to.'

'You would?' His voice went up an octave. 'That's great . . . that's really great. About seven o'clock . . . my place . . .'

My head was still spinning when I walked into the hall. I leaned against the front door, closed my eyes and gave a deep contented sigh. Then I walked into the living room where my parents were watching television.

'Enjoy yourself, darling?' my mother asked.

I nodded dreamily. 'Oh yes, Mum. It was fantastic. . .'

And later, as I sat in my dressing gown, sipping a coffee and absently watching the late-night film, I realised that I hadn't felt so happy in all my life. At last – at long last – all my dreams were coming true.

But that was six months ago, long before Mum began to act so strangely.

*   *   *

The summer had mellowed into glowing autumn, and gradually the golden leaves in the woods above town had withered and fluttered to the ground, until the bare branches were lashed by the biting winds of winter. And though I didn't realise it at the time, that bitterly cold Friday afternoon in February was like a watershed – a moment when my whole life was about to change. I arrived home from school at midday, my hands and face tingling from the blustery gales which had gusted for days. As I'd hurried up the long hill, I'd thought of the piping hot casserole which my father had prepared the previous evening and which even now would be heating up in the oven.

But when I walked into the kitchen, my heart sank. Not only were the vegetables still immersed in pans of cold water, but the gas stove was stone cold. I noticed too that the breakfast dishes hadn't been washed. I paused, leaned against the door and felt my stomach tighten. It could mean only one thing: my mother was ill again.

Knowing exactly what I'd find, I walked into the living room. The curtains were half drawn and my mother was slouched in an armchair in front of the electric fire, the light from the coal-effect panel flickering on the walls of the darkened room. One arm was curled tightly round her frail body; the other held her bowed head, where the dark hair streaked now with grey tumbled untidily over her face. She was so far away, in a nightmare world of her own, that she hadn't even heard me enter.

I stood for a moment, wondering with a growing desperation what I could possibly do to help. Then, gently, I touched her shoulder.

'Are you all right, Mum?' It was a stupid question.

She hadn't been well for months. She jumped and looked up, dazed and startled, and for a few secohds she didn't recognise me.

Her eyelids were red and puffy and the dark circles underneath accentuated her haunted look. She glanced wildly at the clock.

'Oh, Dianne! Is that the time?' She forced herself to her feet, clutching at the table for support. 'I'm sorry, love. I didn't realise it was so late. I'll put the vegetables on.'

'It's no use, Mum. They won't get done in time.' I tried hard to keep the frustration out of my voice. 'Certainly not the casserole. We'll have it tonight instead.'

She began to panic. 'But you must have something warm – especially on a day like today.'

'It's all right. I'll make some chips.'

'But you had chips yesterday.'

'I like chips,' I insisted as I rummaged about in the fridge. 'Besides it wasn't yesterday . . . it was the day before . . .' I brought out a pack of eggs. 'What about an omelette to go with them?'

I made her return to her chair and got on with the task of preparing a hasty lunch. As I beat the eggs, I just couldn't understand the change that had occurred in her. She had become absent-minded, spent most of her time crying, and nagged my father so much that she almost made me scream at times. Fifteen minutes later, I carried two plates into the living room and placed them on the table.

'Come on, Mum,' I announced brightly. 'Lunch is ready . . .'

She moved slowly to the table and sat down. Her lips were tight as she tried to smile. 'Thanks, Dianne, love.

You are a good girl. I don't know what I'd do without you.'

Her words embarrassed me. 'It's nothing, Mum. Please – just eat your food before it gets cold.'

Though my own appetite had almost evaporated, I still managed to eat my lunch. But my mother couldn't. She picked absently with her fork, occasionally forcing down a mouthful as though the food had no taste. She hardly said a word, and I knew she wasn't thinking of me or the food or even what she was doing. Her mind was miles away and the depression she created was a real tangible thing. It seemed to permeate the whole room and the silence became heavy and threatening.

In the end, I couldn't take any more. Gulping down the last chip, I rose abruptly and fled into the kitchen. A few seconds later, she appeared at the door.

'Must take my tablets,' she said vaguely to herself. She squeezed them out of the foil-backed strips, cupped them to her mouth and swallowed them down with a few sips of water.

After she'd returned to the living room, I made a pot of tea and took a cup in to her. She was back in her seat by the fire, her lunch barely touched. She was crying silently and shaking her head as tears trickled uncontrollably down her cheeks. Placing the cup on the table, I knelt beside her and sliding my hand into hers, squeezed it gently.

'Oh, Mum!' Tears now stung my eyes, too. 'Don't you think you ought to see a doctor?'

She closed her eyes tightly and shook her head. 'I have seen him – God knows how many times.'

'Then see him again,' I urged. 'You can't go on like this.'

'What for?' Her voice was muffled. 'I'm taking all

the tablets he's given me . . . I've tried everything. . .everything . . .'

She broke off, her voice stifled by the sobbing that welled up inside her throat.

I felt so inadequate and for several minutes we just sat there, neither of us saying a word. Then, quite suddenly, she looked up. There was desperation in her eyes and her hand gripped mine so fiercely that it hurt.

'Don't go back to school, Dianne. Please . . . take the afternoon off.'

My stomach churned and a lump came to my throat. The thought of spending the whole afternoon with her made me go uptight.

'But I can't, Mum!'

'Oh, please! You must!'

'But my "O" levels – they're less than four months away. I've got so much work . . .'

'Oh, you and your work!' For the first time, anger blazed in her eyes. 'What about me? Don't I matter any more?'

I stood up, hurt and alarmed by the viciousness in her voice. It wasn't true. I did care; more than she could ever know. But there was no way I could have stayed with her at that moment.

'Go then!' she snapped. 'Go if you have to!'

I stared at her, absolutely horrified. She had often shouted at my father like that – but never at me.

'Go!' Her hands were screwed into tight little balls, the knuckles white and prominent. 'Can't you hear? Go!'

I didn't wait. Grabbing my duffel coat, I rushed from the house, leaving the dirty dishes soaking in the sink.

Chapter 2

I didn't stop running until I came to the main road some fifty yards away. And I would have gone on running had it not been for David who was waiting as usual at the corner. Huddled in his dark blue parka jacket, the fur-lined hood pulled up over his head, he had his back turned to the biting wind that whipped in from the sea barely a mile away. When he saw me, his face lit up. But the smile waned when breathlessly I came to a halt beside him.

'Hey! What's up?' His blue eyes were clouded with concern.

I shrugged my shoulders and looked down at the pavement. A sudden gust of wind scattered small dust-devils along the gutter. 'Nothing.'

He frowned. 'It's your mother again, isn't it?' he said gravely.

I paused and nodded, realising it was ridiculous to keep it from him. 'She's worse than usual today,' I said with a sigh.

'I see.' He put his arm around my shoulder as we walked down the road. 'Does that mean you won't be able to come out tonight?'

'Of course not.' I hadn't forgotten it was Friday or that we'd arranged to go to the disco at the youth club. But I had forgotten that my father, who was the manager of one of the largest supermarkets in town, wouldn't be home until late. My heart plummetted to the pit of my stomach.

'I won't be able to come out early though,' I added, realising that I couldn't possibly leave my mother alone again – no matter how I felt. 'I'll have to wait until Dad comes home.'

'That's all right by me. I could come round to your place if you like. Keep you company?'

I thought quickly. There wasn't anything I'd like better, but with my mother in her present condition, it would be much too embarrassing. 'No. Better not,' I replied with a quick shake of the head. 'I'd better phone you when Dad gets in – though it probably won't be till after eight.'

If my curt reply hurt, he didn't show it. 'Fair enough. I've got plenty of work to do. I should get on with some revision, I suppose.'

So we agreed that I should phone him as soon as Dad arrived home. I felt so much better now that I was with David – he always had that effect on me. But as we sauntered down the hill and the school came into sight – a long modern building made almost entirely of concrete and glass – I couldn't help thinking how unfair life was.

'Do you think it's worth it?' I asked suddenly.

His brow wrinkled with bewilderment. 'What is?'

'All this work we have to do. Staying in almost every night . . . worrying about what's likely to come up in the exams. I mean . . . where's it going to get us?'

He grinned wryly. 'To university . . . if we're lucky.'

I looked up at him. He was exactly two years and one month older than me and in the second year of the sixth form. In just a few short months he'd be sitting his 'A' levels.

'I know. But is it worth the aggro? Think of all the others who have opted out. Are they really any worse off than we are? If anything they seem to get more out of life than we do. At least, they don't have to think twice before going to a disco or pop concert. If they've got the money, they just go.'

This time he laughed. 'I know what you mean. But it's a question I daren't ask myself.'

'Why not?'

He shrugged his shoulders. 'In case I pack it all in . . .'

'There. You more or less admit it. It isn't worth it.'

'Hold on. I haven't finished yet . . .' He shook his head slowly. 'It is really — when you consider everything. I suppose I could leave right now and get myself a job in an office, but I wouldn't be happy.'

Reluctantly, I had to agree. I didn't want to work in an office either and the thought of being cooped up in a factory made my blood run cold. But the way work was piling up at school was getting me down. The pressures were far too intense.

Then David broke into my thoughts. 'You know what your trouble is, don't you? Your mother. Having her so ill must be making things really difficult . . .'

I gave a deep sigh. He was right. But knowing what the problem was didn't solve it — or make it any more bearable — and I wondered how much more I could take without cracking up. By this time, we had reached the school gates and the bell was ringing.

'Don't let it get you down.' David gripped my arm and gave it a gentle squeeze. 'Look on the bright side. Think of the summer when the exams are over. We'll be able to spend every day on the beach, just soaking up the sun.'

I smiled up at him, remembering last year's barbecue. 'Yes!' I admitted, quickly thrusting out the de-
pressing thought that we'd be waiting for our results.
'That will be great.'

'I'm glad to hear it,' he replied with a mock severity
that made me giggle. 'So now perhaps we'll have less of
all this gloomy talk.' He looked down and grinned,
adding gently, 'Don't worry too much about your
mother, Dianne. She'll get better — just you wait and
see.'

I nodded — and wondered just how long it would be.

Fondly, I watched him stride across the yard to the
sixth form common room at the rear of the school. I
had known him for as long as I could remember, which
wasn't surprising, seeing that ours is a small seaside
town where everyone seems to know everyone else.
Yet it was difficult to believe that it was only six
months since we'd become such close friends. Then I
realised that within another six months, if he got the
right grades, he'd be leaving for university. The
thought made me sad. I turned and hurried across the
girls' yard, past the large assembly hall with its six
flights of steps that led to a semi-circular foyer and,
entering the main building, mounted a maze of stairs
and corridors to my form room on the top floor.

Erica waved as I walked in and I joined her at the
rear of the classroom where she was hugging the
radiator.

'Have you heard the news?' she asked, moving over
to let me share the warmth. 'We won't be going to the
youth club disco tonight after all.'

I looked at her in surprise. 'Why ever not? Don't tell
me it's all over between you and Bob.'

Her forehead puckered in a frown, which had the

strange effect of making her seem prettier than ever. 'Of course it isn't!' she replied with a perplexed shake of the head. 'Whatever gave you that idea?'

'You did. When you said you wouldn't be going to the disco.'

She gave an impatient snort. 'I didn't mean that. I meant that the disco's been cancelled.'

'Oh no!' I'd really been looking forward to going, even though it would only have been for the last hour or so. 'What's happened? Is Mr Saunders ill or something?'

Mr Saunders was the warden of the youth club, a young enthusiastic teacher with a short dark beard and who seemed to possess only one pair of jeans and an infinite supply of patience.

Erica shook her head. 'Haven't you heard? About Jago Brown?'

I rolled my eyes. 'Who hasn't heard of Jago Brown?'

'Well, there was a fight last night . . . between him and some other guy . . . so Mr Saunders decided to cancel.'

'That's a bit drastic, isn't it?'

'That's what I thought. But apparently, this other guy is a member of a gang from the other side of town . . . and the rumour's been going round that he and his mates are coming across tonight.'

'Trust them. And I was really looking forward to going out with David.'

'Not to worry. We can go down to Joe's instead.'

Joe's was a small cafe on the promenade where most of us met when we had nowhere better to go.

At that moment, a voice came from behind me. 'Are you really? Mind if I join you?'

I didn't have to turn to know who it was. Stacy

Heatherington had a smooth sultry voice, all put on of course, which seemed to match her well-developed figure. She'd even had her hair specially cut and lightened so that it tumbled provocatively down one side of her face.

You'd swear that she was about to enter a beauty contest. But it wasn't merely the fact that she made me feel so dowdy that made me dislike her. She was always hanging around David and it didn't take a genius to realise she fancied him.

Erica answered for me. 'As long as you bring your own boyfriend.' Obviously she didn't trust her with Bob either.

'Of course.' Stacy was haughty now, stung by the implied insult. 'What time?'

'Seven o'clock,' I replied, quite maliciously, knowing that it would be at least nine before we arrived there. With a bit of luck, she'd have gone by then.

'Great. See you there.'

At that moment, Miss Paige, our form tutor, came in. She banged her register on the desk and called for silence. Not everybody heard her so she had to call again before the din eventually subsided.

'Thank you.' She sat down and proceeded to call out our names. When she'd finished she stood up. 'You may have your English essays back.' She indicated the pile of blue exercise books in front of her. 'We'll discuss them when we meet later this afternoon. Don't all rush. I'm sure you're dying to find out how well you've done.'

She sailed out of the room, her black gown billowing out behind her, and left us to the half-hearted scramble for the books. I had a quick glance at mine before leaving for the first lesson; an hour of netball with Miss Ware, our games mistress. C plus. Not bad. But it wasn't as good as my usual B or A minus, and I wondered as I crossed the yard to the gymnasium what Miss Paige was going to say.

Miss Ware was waiting for us outside the changing rooms. Dressed in an immaculate grey tracksuit with red piping along the seams and with her blonde hair cut conveniently short, she oozed authority and confidence. Though barely ten years older than us, she was one of the most respected teachers in the school.

'Get dressed quickly, girls,' she commanded as she opened the door. 'And no talking.'

We all grinned as we trooped in. We knew from experience that her bark was far worse than her bite. Within minutes we had changed and picking up the dozen balls from the large wooden box at one end of the gym, made our way to the courts at the rear of the school. They were really tennis courts but in winter, with the nets stored away, they doubled for netball.

Miss Ware came hurrying along behind us. As she entered through a gate in the high fence, she blew sharply on the whistle which was slung on a leather thong around her neck.

'Right. Put the balls in the centre circle; then stand on the sidelines.' She clapped her hands together twice. 'Come on, girls. Quietly.'

Nobody ever thought of cheeking her. Obediently, we did as we were told and the warming-up session began. I was a member of the senior netball team and Miss Ware had always stressed the importance of the warming-up period, so not wishing to lose my place through a pulled muscle, I went meticulously through the exercises. First we ran the length of the courts and back, though of course Stacy managed to get away with going half-way and then mingling unobtrusively with the rest of us as we returned.

Then came the running, turning and passing exercises when we grouped into threes: myself, Erica, and a girl called Sharon Pearson who had the reputation of being a drop-out. After about five minutes of passing and throwing, we were ready for the game.

Miss Ware split us into four groups and sent us with our bibs to opposite ends of the courts. Erica, Stacy and I were put in the same team and presented with red bibs. But when Stacy received hers, she tossed back her long fair hair.

'But Miss, it clashes with my colour scheme,' she complained, holding the bib against her cerise tracksuit.

Miss Ware turned, hands on hips, and glared at her, while the rest of us laughed spontaneously. Which naturally didn't please Stacy at all.

'Well it does clash, Miss,' she said petulantly, and hiding her embarrassment, walked to the centre circle, tucking her long hair into an elastic band.

For the next three quarters of an hour, we played netball with enthusiasm, practising our moves and tactics with Miss Ware yelling orders and encouragement – as well as frequent admonitions – so that the time flew. All too soon, we were trotting breathlessly back to the changing rooms for a welcome shower.

I felt much better as I made my way back to my form room for the last lesson of the day. All my tensions had been washed away and I was ready to face any criticism which Miss Paige might throw at me.

She came in, armed with her marking register and a file in which she kept her notes. 'Now then. Those essays,' she said ominously.

Actually, she didn't say much – except to point out that my essay wasn't up to my usual standard. Then she told us to take out our set book, *Cider with Rosie*, and asked us one by one to read aloud.

Then suddenly, as I glanced out of the window, my eyes were drawn to our estate on the hill overlooking the school. It was barely a mile away, surrounded on two sides by a belt of trees which seemed to be casting a skeletal arm around the fifty or so houses. I could even see my own house; the late afternoon sun suddenly appearing from behind leaden skies flashed on the windows of my bedroom. I thought of my mother, lying in her bed crying or, if the tablets had worked, mercifully asleep.

And as I thought of her, my stomach went into a tight knot. It was a strange inexplicable feeling, but at that moment I had a kind of premonition that all was not well at home. That somehow my mother needed help. I felt my whole body go cold and tense; my hands went cold and clammy and I felt physically sick. I closed my eyes and gulped hard.

I became aware that Miss Paige was talking to me.

'Dianne Barrett!' Her voice was sharp. 'I've asked you to read.'

I glanced up in confusion. 'I'm sorry, Miss. What was that?'

She rolled her eyes in despair. 'Haven't you heard a word I've said? Honestly, Dianne. I don't know what's come over you recently. You're not here half the time. At least, not in spirit.'

I mumbled an apology.

'I asked you to read from the top of page twenty-seven.' She walked to my desk, glanced at my book, and gave a gasp of annoyance.

My book wasn't even open at the right page.

'I think you'd better see me later, my girl,' she said. 'After the others have left.'

There were a few sniggers, but she turned abruptly. 'If you think it's funny, Stacy Heatherington, perhaps you can show us how to do it properly.'

I felt such a fool being shown up in front of everybody, but I was glad she hadn't asked me to read. It would only have made matters worse. The way I felt at that moment, I would have made a real mess of it. The minutes ticked slowly by and the nasty feeling grew, making me more and more anxious about my mother.

Eventually, the bell rang for the end of the afternoon, but Miss Paige took no notice of it. She insisted we read to the very end of the chapter before dismissing us. Everyone made a dash for the door, and I sidled out with them, hoping that she had forgotten. I should have known better; she had a memory that could out-elephant elephants.

'Not you, Dianne Barrett. I want to see you. Remember?'

I stood in front of her desk while she arranged the books into neat piles. She was being deliberately, annoyingly slow. Eventually, she sat back in her chair and looked up.

'Now then, Dianne. What on earth's got into you recently?'

Now that everyone had left, her voice was gentle, the concern evident in her eyes. She shook her head slowly, and a solitary ray of sunshine, slanting weakly through a gap in the clouds, made the auburn highlights flash in her dark brown hair. 'Your work has deteriorated so much lately, I can hardly believe it. You're one of my

25

best students. What's happened to you?'

She stopped, waiting for a reply. I shrugged my shoulders. How could I possibly tell her about my mother? It wasn't the sort of thing anyone would like to talk about. And besides, how was I going to explain something I didn't really understand?

'Is there anything wrong at home?' she asked patiently.

I didn't say anything. I knew instinctively that Miss Paige was someone I could trust. Though she was strict, she could also be very understanding. And I desperately needed to talk to someone older. But not at that moment.

'Because if there is,' she continued, 'I'd like to help.'

I thought of my mother again. The peculiar feeling grew stronger and my stomach went into spasms once more. I had to get home quickly.

'Please, Miss. I know I should have been listening.' My voice sounded strange as though it wasn't coming from me. 'But you see . . . I have to get home . . .'

Some of my desperation must have transmitted itself to her because she frowned and gave a worried tight-lipped smile. 'Very well, Dianne. But remember; you've only got another four months. And you could get 'A' grades if you work hard.' She paused and emphasised her words. 'But you can't afford to waste any time.'

She was right. I couldn't afford to waste any time at all. But not in the sense she meant.

I couldn't get out of school fast enough. I wished now that I hadn't left my mother alone – and the guilt churned inside me. As I burst through the swing doors into the yard, I discovered David sitting on one of the wooden benches around the ornamental pool. He glanced up in surprise as I dashed towards him.

'I can't wait,' I exclaimed before he could utter even a word. 'I've got to get home.'

'Hold on. Wait for me.' He caught me up before I'd taken half a dozen steps. 'I'll come with you.'

He didn't bother to ask me why I was in such a desperate hurry.

Together we plunged along, spurring up the steep tree-lined avenue, half-running, half-walking, until I was gasping for breath. I felt the cold air rasp in my throat. But no matter how hard I pushed forward, my legs felt like lead weights and I seemed hardly to be moving.

But at last we reached the corner that led into the cul-de-sac at the end of which stood our house.

I stopped dead, and putting a hand to my lips, gave a sharp cry. For there at the end was an ambulance. I heard the metallic slam of a closing door and saw the small cluster of anxious neighbours. Then the driver appeared from the rear and with a deceptive calmness mounted into his seat. With blue lights flashing, he pulled away. By the time he reached us, the siren was screaming its urgent message.

Everything seemed to whirl around me and desperately I gripped David's arm. Silent tears streamed uncontrollably down my face. I knew without having to be told that my mother was in that ambulance. That something terrible had happened to her. Something I could have so easily prevented.

Chapter 3

As I watched the ambulance disappear around a bend in the road, it was as though I were some other person; I couldn't believe that all this was happening to me. My mind was in a whirl and I was so confused that all I could do was stand and stare long after the vehicle had gone out of sight. At least, it seemed a long time. I felt a hand on my shoulder and when I turned, I found that Mrs Judd, our next-door neighbour, was standing at my side. Older than my parents, with a grown-up family who had already left home, she had been a very good friend to my mother for several years.

'Come on, Dianne!' she said gently. 'You'd better come with me.'

I didn't really hear her – the words didn't register – and when she tried to lead me to her house, I pulled away.

'But my mother,' I cried desperately. 'She's in that ambulance, isn't she?'

'Yes, she is. But she's all right.' Mrs Judd's voice was calm and soothing. 'Come inside – I can explain better there.' And when I began to resist, she went on, 'Your mother's in no danger. Honestly, she isn't . . .'

I allowed her to lead me up the path, alongside which small bunches of early daffodils were beginning to bloom. As she opened the door, I suddenly remembered David. When I turned he waved.

'See you later,' he called.

I waved back absently and followed Mrs Judd inside.

'Now then!' she said, smiling yet business-like. 'Let's make ourselves a cup of tea, shall we?'

But my reply was blunt. 'I'd rather know what's happened to my mother.'

She didn't take offence. 'Of course you would.' But even so, she insisted on putting on the kettle first. 'Right. Now let's go into the living room.'

She sat opposite me on a plush red armchair, her hands folded over her knees. 'As I said, Dianne, your mother's in no danger. That I can promise you.'

'But what happened? Please tell me.'

'Well . . .' she began. 'As you know, your mother hasn't been well for months. Anyway, this afternoon, about three-quarters of an hour ago, she came knocking at the door. She was all – woozy, I suppose you'd call it – and said she was feeling terrible. Of course, I brought her in and telephoned the doctor . . .'

'Yes. But what had she done?'

'Well – she'd taken an overdose of tablets.' She went on hurriedly. 'It wasn't deliberate . . . I know it wasn't. It's just that she got confused and couldn't remember exactly how many she'd taken.'

Guilt flooded through me and when I spoke it was a mere whisper. 'You are . . . you are telling me the truth?'

'Oh, Dianne. I wouldn't lie to you. Not about something as important as this.' When she saw how upset I was, she sat beside me on the settee, and putting her arm round my shoulder, cradled me to her. 'And do you honestly believe that if your mother was in any danger that I'd keep you here talking like this? Why!

29

We'd be driving after that ambulance this very minute.'

'My father. Does he know?'

'Of course. I phoned him while the doctor was here. He told me where the tablets were and exactly how many of them should be left. All she'd taken was enough to make her sleep, that's all. And it was an accident, Dianne.'

She gave me some tissues and I wiped my eyes. 'Now. Let's have that cup of tea, shall we?'

She stood up, leaving me alone for a few minutes. A sudden gusting shower splattered against the window pane with a rattle that made me jump. I glanced out at the dark clouds, heavy with rain, that raced across the sky, and shivered. I shouldn't have left her alone, I kept telling myself; I should have listened to her.

Presently, Mrs Judd returned with a tray and poured the tea. I nibbled a chocolate biscuit half-heartedly and thought of Dad.

'Where's my father now?' I asked.

'He's down at the hospital. He went there straight from work. Would you like to be there with him?'

I didn't have to be asked twice. 'Yes – I think I'd like to. If you don't mind.'

'Of course I don't mind.' She gave me a smile. 'It's only natural you should want to be with your mother at a time like this. Though I'm going to tell you again –' she called from the hall as she went to get her coat ' – she's in no danger . . . no danger at all.'

Mrs Judd insisted on driving me to the hospital even though I could quite easily have caught a bus, and within a quarter of an hour we were there. She drove through a narrow opening where once wrought-iron gates had barred the way and pulled into the car park. It was so small it must have been planned in an era when cars were few and far between. She got out and locked the door behind her.

'I'll just make sure your father's here before I leave you,' she said, leading me to the Emergency and Accident Department. It was jammed between the old stone-built administrative block and the newer red-brick out-patients' department. There was a young nurse behind the sliding glass window who asked us to take a seat in the waiting room. It had just gone five o'clock and the only occupants of the waiting room, which was cluttered with small low tables and vinyl armchairs, were an old couple in a far corner, and my father. Above him, on the magnolia-coloured walls, was a large clock which gave a loud click as the minute hand jerked to the five-minute mark.

He was hunched on the edge of his chair, his elbows resting heavily on his legs, his body bent forward. Both hands were over his face.

'I'll leave you now,' Mrs Judd whispered. 'But if you need anything, just give me a ring. And you won't forget to let me know how your mother is, will you?'

I walked towards my father and even before I reached him, he seemed to sense I was there because he looked up. His face was grey and his eyes had lines of worry radiating from them. He stood up, looked at me for a moment and then held out his arms. I rushed into them and putting my head against his shoulder, began to cry.

'Hey. Come on, Dianne. Don't cry. Everything's all right.' He made me sit down and handed me his hand-kerchief. 'You should have stayed at home. There's nothing you can do here.'

'But Dad. Don't you understand? I wanted to come.' My voice was hoarse as a lump rose into my throat and almost prevented me from speaking. 'I couldn't stay in the house . . . waiting . . . wondering . . .'

'No, of course not.' A smile flickered briefly on his lips as he took my hand and squeezed it. 'Anyway, we shouldn't be long. I'm just waiting to see the doctor. He said he'd be out of the ward by five o'clock . . .'

We both glanced at the clock above us. It was ten past.

'He shouldn't be long now.'

There was a moment's silence while I tried to pluck up courage to ask the question which had been plaguing me.

'What . . . what exactly happened?'

He looked up. 'Didn't Mrs Judd tell you?'

'Yes – but I didn't know whether to believe her. You see . . .'

'You see what?'

I shrugged my shoulders. 'I wondered if . . .' I let the words trail away, afraid to utter them.

'You wondered if your mother took a deliberate overdose,' he asked, and when I nodded, went on. 'No. It was accidental, all right. For months now, I've been looking after her tablets; doctor's orders. I gave her just enough to last the day.' He gave a deep sigh. 'It seems she took them all at one go – at least most of them – and of course when she began to feel queer, she got scared. It was lucky that Mrs Judd was at home or goodness knows what would have happened.'

At that moment, a coloured doctor came through the swing doors and asked my father to follow him.

Dad squeezed my hand once more. 'Won't be long,' he said.

As I watched him go, I had to bite my lip to stop the tears which were beginning to sting my eyes again. I loved my mother, but I loved my father more. I always had. Ever since I could remember, we'd got on well together. In a way, I suppose it was natural. My mother had often been ill, and he had had to be both a father and a mother to me at times. And of course whenever my mother had been depressed, he went out of his way to compensate for it, making me laugh and trying to dispel the gloom which descended on our house.

It was natural I should care for someone who showed me so much love.

And as I watched him follow the doctor into the office, I couldn't help feeling bitter towards my mother for the way she was making him suffer. It wasn't right that one human being should do that to another.

It was almost half-past five when he emerged, and his face was serious, his forehead furrowed with a deep frown. I stood up anxiously.

'What is it, Dad? Is she all right?'

He nodded vaguely, deep in thought. 'Yes – yes, of course she is. But there's been another development, I'm afraid. It just so happened that the psychiatrist was here this afternoon – it was his weekly clinic. Anyway, he's been to see your mother . . .' He hesitated and bit his lip. 'He wants her to go into his hospital for a few weeks.'

There was suddenly a large hole in the pit of my stomach and I felt sick. 'He wants her to go into a mental hospital?'

'Yes, Dianne. I'm afraid so,' he said.

'I see. And when is she going to . . . to this other hospital?' I couldn't bring myself to call it by its proper name.

'He wants her to go tomorrow. As soon as she's fit to travel.'

Then, aware that the old man and woman were listening, he led me to the door. 'Let's go home,' he whispered. 'We can discuss it better there.'

We drove home in silence, but even when we arrived, neither of us wanted to talk. We tidied the place, washing up the dirty plates left from breakfast and lunch, and ran the hoover quickly over the living room. I was too embarrassed to mention the matter and yet I knew the time would come when we could delay it no longer.

My father, reading my thoughts, said, 'You're worried, aren't you? About your mother going into a mental hospital.' After I'd nodded, he went on. 'You mustn't be. There's no stigma to it these days.' He told me about some statistics he'd read, but though I didn't say so, I knew that statistics didn't matter. What people thought, did. And I dreaded the idea of our neighbours whispering behind our backs. Especially the girls at school.

I changed the subject abruptly and suggested a Chinese meal instead of the casserole we should have had for lunch. To my relief he agreed, and went out in his car to the take-away.

Later, we sat at opposite ends of the table and ate in silence. Then my father looked up. 'I think we ought to plan exactly what we're going to do,' he said. 'The next few weeks are going to be difficult. Dr Stevenson says your mother could be there for a couple of months . . .'

I felt suddenly sick. 'Dr Stevenson?'

'The psychiatrist. He reckoned it might take some time for your mother to make a complete recovery.'

'But she will – make a complete recovery, I mean?'

He nodded. 'Of course. It all depends on how she responds to treatment. So . . . I'm afraid we're going to have to get ourselves organised.'

'I could have a snack in the school canteen,' I suggested. 'Or take sandwiches.'

Though it hadn't escaped my mind that sandwiches had to be prepared beforehand — which might make more work.

'Great. I could do the same,' he said, taking a sip of wine. 'Of course we'll have to prepare our evening meal the night before. I could do the vegetables — and I could get one of the girls at work to do my shopping for me. We do it for some of our customers, so it won't be a hardship.'

'And I could do the cooking when I arrive home,' I added.

'Think you can manage?'

'Of course I can.' I didn't tell him that I'd been doing just that for ages. 'That's no problem.'

'Very well. That leaves the cleaning and washing. If we try to keep everything up to date — keep the place as tidy as possible — we can do most of the work at week-ends. But . . .' He looked up. 'If you find things getting on top of you, promise you'll tell me.'

'Oh, Dad. Don't be ridiculous!' I forced a note of brightness into my voice. 'We'll manage all right. I know we will. I mean, there'll only be the two of us.'

He gave a slow grin. 'Yes, I know. But it's just as well to be careful. After all, you've got your 'O' levels this year. I don't want you to jeopardise your chances, do I?'

I had to agree though I declined to mention that all this had happened at the most awkward time. We then discussed further what we were going to do, but as we were washing up I decided to tell him what had been troubling me all evening.

'Dad . . .' I began and broke off, trying to find the right words.

He must have realised that I had something important to say. 'Come on,' he said. 'Out with it. We've ne r had any secrets from each other. Let's not start now.'

'About what happened today.' I put the plate I was wiping into the rack. 'I think . . . I think I was partly to blame.'

'What are you talking about?' He frowned and flicked the soapy water from his hands before drying them. 'How do you work that out?'

'Well, you see . . . Mum asked me, begged me to stay home this afternoon and . . . and I refused. If I'd been here, all this wouldn't have occurred.'

Now that it was out in the open, I felt relieved. But my father shook his head. 'That's ridiculous. You can't hold yourself responsible. You're right in a way. If you had stayed home, it probably wouldn't have happened. But you couldn't possibly stay home every day, and it would surely have happened some other time. But she didn't take those tablets deliberately, you know. She told the doctor so herself.' He put his arm round my shoulder. 'So you can put that idea right out of your mind.'

I dried my eyes. 'Do you mean that?'

'Of course I do. Besides, she would have had to go into hospital some time. She couldn't have gone on as she was, could she?'

As we walked back into the living room, I realised how right he was.

'No! It isn't your fault,' he continued, and now there was a serious thoughtful expression in his eyes. 'If anyone is to blame, it's me!'

I didn't think anything of that remark at the time. But later – much later – I was to remember the words clearly. And know the terrible effect they were to have on me.

Chapter 4

By eight-thirty, we were drinking our usual cup of coffee, and my father had helped himself to a large brandy. It was strange to be sitting there in the living room, just the two of us, talking. Normally there was an indefinable air of tension as my mother huddled in her favourite chair as though it gave her a peculiar kind of protection. She was hardly ever out of that chair. Now that she wasn't with us, the atmosphere was different. The lights seemed strangely brighter and as I looked at the reproduction of Constable's *Haywain* on the wall opposite, I could swear that the colours were unusually vivid. It was a disturbing sensation – as though all the gloom had been plucked away and I was seeing things as they were meant to be seen. I realised with a simultaneous sense of shame that I was glad Mum wasn't with us.

Dad glanced at his watch. 'Aren't you going out tonight?' he asked. He was stretched out in his arm-chair, totally at ease for the first time in weeks, and I couldn't help noticing that in spite of the grey hair around his temples, he was quite young-looking for his age.

'As a matter of fact, David said he was going to call round,' I replied. It was only then that I remembered that I'd arranged to phone him. Or had I? I couldn't remember clearly. I said so to Dad.

'You'd better go ahead and do it, hadn't you?'

I hesitated. 'I'm not sure I ought to go out,' I said.

'Why ever not?'

'Because Mum's in hospital, of course.'

But he didn't agree with me.

'I think you should go out,' he said solemnly. 'I think it's important that we should live our lives as near to normal as possible.'

'Perhaps you're right,' I conceded.

'I know I'm right. Now why don't you phone that young man of yours?'

But as I made my way to the telephone in the hall, there was a knock on the front door. I opened it and found David standing there; a couple of feet behind him, as though they were too bashful to come nearer, were Erica and Bob.

'Hi!' David gave me a shy smile. 'When you didn't phone me, I wondered how things were . . .'

'Yes,' said Erica, coming nearer. 'We heard about your mother and thought we should come over to see how she is.'

I shrugged my shoulders and stood aside to let them in. 'She's all right,' I said, and explained briefly what had happened.

'I'm glad,' said David with a sigh of relief. 'We were told she was seriously ill.'

I shook my head. 'No. She's all right . . . except. . .well, I suppose you'd better know; she's going to be in hospital for several weeks.'

They were all sympathetic as I showed them into the

lounge. Too sympathetic when I told them that she was going to be admitted into a psychiatric hospital the next day. I couldn't help thinking that if she were suffering from a physical complaint, though they'd still be sympathetic, there would be no embarrassment lurking under the surface.

'Not to worry, Dianne,' said Erica in a vain attempt to console me. 'She's in the best place.'

I ignored it. How would she feel if it were her mother? I wondered.

'Well, now we're here,' David said as he sat on the arm of one of the light green Dralon-covered chairs. If Mum had seen him do that, she'd have been furious. 'What would you like to do? Shall we go out? Or shall we stay in?'

I shook my head decisively now that my father had made me change my mind. 'No. I think I'd prefer to go out.'

'Suits us,' said Bob. He was standing near the door, his tall angular body almost touching the top of the frame. 'But where? It's either the youth club or Joe's . . .'

'The youth club's closed,' I pointed out.

Erica shook her head. 'Wrong. Mr Saunders has changed his mind. He's having the disco after all. He's just banned Jago, that's all.'

I thought of the crowded hall and smoke-filled lounge. 'I think I'd prefer Joe's,' I said.

'Joe's it is then,' said Bob, grinning, his bright auburn hair flashing in the light. 'And since my old man gave me an extra pound this week, the first drink's on me.'

'We'll keep you to that,' promised David, leading the way into the living room to say good evening to my father. Then a few minutes later after I'd run quickly upstairs to get my thick coat and fur-lined mittens, we were tumbling out of the front door.

'Better take your key,' called my father as we left. 'I may go out later – depends how I feel.'

The wind had dropped as we strolled down the long meandering road into town. The low clouds which had scudded so wildly across the heavens that afternoon had given way to a starry sky. A full moon made it appear almost as light as day.

It was great being with David. He put his arm round my shoulder and I huddled up to him to keep warm for though the wind had eased, it was still icy cold. He made me feel so safe and as we ambled along, looking down on the town, the roofs of its houses almost white against the dark impenetrable shadows, it was as though we were in another world.

He stopped suddenly and made me face him. 'Promise me something, Dianne,' he said sombrely.

I looked up. 'Of course. What?'

'I know it's not going to be easy, your mother being in hospital. So – if you every need any help, promise you'll tell me.'

'Oh, David.' His words made a lump come into my throat. 'I'll be all right.'

'Perhaps you will. But promise me anyway.'

'Of course I promise,' I whispered.

'Great.' He brought his head down and kissed me so lightly that my lips actually tingled. 'Now don't forget it. Any time you need me, I'll be there.'

At that moment, someone called from lower down the hill. 'Are you two going to stay there all night?' It was Bob, yelling as only Bob knew how to yell. I was sure he could be heard all over town.

'We're coming,' shouted David in reply. Then looking at me, he said, 'We'd better get a move on. Or they'll start thinking all sorts of things.'

Together, hand in hand, we ran laughing down the hill so that by the time we reached Erica and Bob we were completely out of breath.

We hurried through the deserted centre of the old town, a square bounded on one side by the railway station, on another by the seafront hotels, while the remaining two sides were taken up by short rows of shops selling gifts and ice-cream. In the centre was the open-air market, its stalls now bleak and empty. We were protected in the streets, but as soon as we turned on to the prom, the strong sea breeze cut through my thick coat. By the time I arrived at Joe's, a mere hundred yards away, I was frozen stiff.

The lace-curtained windows were steamed up and as soon as we opened the door, the warmth came out to welcome us like a thick blanket. It was only half full and we found a table as far away from the door as we could. David and Bob went to the counter to get the coffees, leaving Erica and me alone for a few minutes.

'Look, Dianne,' she began as soon as we'd settled down, 'I know you've been having a rough time lately, but if there's anything I can do to help – anything – you only have to ask, you know.'

I thought of David's identical offer and realised how lucky I was to have such good friends.

'Thanks, Erica. But quite honestly, I'm not sure what you could do.'

'Well, I could give you a hand with the weekly wash and the ironing for a start . . .' She gave her usual grimace. 'Though I don't promise not to scorch anything. And I know I wouldn't be any good at your father's shirts, but – hey!' Her eyes brightened as an idea occurred to her. 'I've just thought of something. Perhaps my mother will do them for you. She's a dab hand at ironing.'

She made me laugh. 'Oh, great. You offer to help and land your mother with some work she could probably do without. Anyhow, Dad and I can manage quite well, thanks. You seem to forget that my mother has been ill on and off for some time. We've had to learn to fend for ourselves.'

'I realise that.' Once bitten by an idea she was reluctant to let go. 'But there must be something I can do. I surely could help with the cleaning.'

That – I had to admit – was a good idea, seeing how much I hated it. 'OK. You could come round on Sunday mornings and give me a hand with the dusting – and peeling the vegetables, if you like . . .'

She frowned cautiously. 'Sunday mornings? Er . . .what time? Only I like to have a lie-in on a Sunday.'

Honestly, she was impossible. 'You don't have to come round too early. Eleven o'clock will do.'

She thought for a moment. 'Yes. I should be awake by then. If I'm not, just put the duster in my hand and point me in the right direction.'

The guys came back, each carrying two large steaming mugs of welcome coffee.

'I've just been telling Dianne,' Erica said with unwarranted enthusiasm as she cradled the mug in her hands, 'we'll give her all the help she needs. All she has to do is say the word.'

It was just like Erica to organise everyone – and probably end up doing nothing herself. And of course David and Bob were only too ready to agree with her.

'You know you can come over to my place for a meal any time you like,' said David.

There was an animated discussion during which they were busy organising my life. In the end, I just had to interrupt.

'You all seem to be forgetting one thing,' I protested as soon as I could get a word in. 'Our exams. I have an idea we're all going to be pretty busy soon.'

'True. But many hands make light work,' David pointed out. 'And it would give you more time for revision, wouldn't it?'

'I know. But let's not forget that my father will have something to say about this. Thanks a lot, but I'm sure we'll be able to manage all right. Though – ' I realised just how ungracious my words sounded '– if I'm ever in an emergency, I'll know where to come, won't I?'

At that moment, the door flew open and a strong breeze gusted in, scattering some paper napkins on a nearby table. And with it came Jago Brown. I don't know why it was, but every time I saw him, I cringed – I couldn't stand to be near him. He was tall with dark greasy hair and dressed in a black leather motor-cycling outfit studded with gleaming metal. On the back of his jacket was painted a white skull and crossbones with the word 'Jago' above, and below, the word 'Rules'. He obviously wanted everyone to know who he was. I think it was his arrogance more than anything that made me feel such revulsion.

He paused inside the door and pulled off his gauntlets. Then he saw us and giving a huge grin, which I imagined was supposed to show he was in one of his friendly moods, weaved his way through the tables towards us. He was followed by a girl in leather gear and a gormless-looking fellow called Kenny

Chapman who followed him around so much, he was almost like his shadow.

'Oh no,' I muttered. 'Here comes trouble.'

The others looked up. My heart sank when David gave him a cheery wave and asked him to join us. Jago pulled a chair from another table and sat across it cowboy fashion.

'What you doing down here then?' He plonked his helmet in the middle of the table. 'Thought you went to the youth club of a Friday night.'

'We decided not to go tonight,' I replied coldly. 'We thought there might be trouble there. Like last night.'

My sarcasm was lost on him. 'Yeah. Rotten business that. And all because of them yobs from the Greenfield estate.'

I looked at him in amazement. Here was the self-styled King of the Yobs. Talk about calling the kettle black.

'The way I heard it, you had something to do with it too.'

This time the self-confident smile faded. 'Perhaps I did. But what would you do if someone insulted your mother?'

David nudged my knee with his. 'That gang came down looking for trouble,' he said with more than a trace of embarrassment in his voice. 'I heard that Jago took a load of goading before he thumped the guy.'

'You can say that again.' It was the girl who spoke, and up till then I hadn't recognised her. It was Sharon Pearson who that afternoon had been practising netball with us. And it wasn't any wonder that I didn't recognise her — she was dressed all in black and wearing make-up so thick you could have scraped it off with a knife. She stood with one hand on her hip and the other resting on Jago's shoulder. 'They kept on picking on him, didn't they?'

'Yeah. Picking on him,' repeated Kenny in a thick muffled voice and punching one hand into the palm of the other.

'So what else could he do?' she went on. 'He had to belt one of them, didn't he? And I know 'cos I was there. Not like some people.'

'Not like some people,' said Kenny inevitably.

Erica and Bob had been sitting quietly, but now Bob spoke. 'Sharon's right. Jago was forced into that scrap – and ended up getting blamed for it.'

'And getting banned from the youth club for a month,' Jago added glumly. 'Now what am I going to do during the day . . . what with no job to go to.' He paused and thought. 'Don't suppose you can blame old Saunders though. Has to keep me away till the din dies down.'

His admission startled me, but it did nothing to change my feelings.

None of us had noticed Joe, the proprietor himself, coming over. He tapped Jago on the shoulder. 'Right you,' he said gruffly. 'Out.'

Jago looked up, a mixture of surprise and indignation on his face. 'Why? I haven't done nothing.'

Joe was a big man with thick hairy arms and a chest that bulged under a tight pullover. Rumour had it that once he had wrestled on television, though no one could really remember him. He made Jago look small and puny.

'I said "out". Are you going on your own two feet? Or do I have to sling you out?'

With arms like his, he could have thrown all of us out at one go.

Jago shrugged his shoulders, gave us a wave, and with a contemptuous smile on his lips, swaggered to the door, followed by Joe.

Joe closed the door firmly and then turned and looked at us. For a moment, I thought he was going to throw us out too. But he returned instead to the counter and began washing up some cups and saucers.

I breathed a sigh of relief. 'Thank goodness he's gone.'

'What, Jago?' David gave a grin. 'He's all right really. When you get to know him.'

'All right!' The words came out much louder than I intended and some people at a far table looked round. 'How can you possibly say such a thing?' I continued in a low voice. 'After all the trouble he's caused in his time?'

'We'd have all been in trouble if we'd had the kind of home life he's had,' said Bob. To my surprise, Erica agreed with him.

'What do you mean?' I asked doubtfully.

'If your father had gone off one night when you were nine or ten and you never saw him again,' David said quietly. 'Then perhaps we would all have kicked over the traces too.'

'And having a succession of "uncles" doesn't help either,' added Bob.

There was a brief silence. 'Perhaps we should be sorry for him,' mused Erica.

I shook my head. Sorry? I thought. Be sorry for Jago Brown? When would Jago ever feel sorry for anyone?

'How come you know so much about him anyway?' I asked David, the coldness still in my voice. 'I wouldn't have thought you'd ever have much to do with him.'

David laughed. 'It's just that we were in the same

form once.'

'Jago in the top form? I don't believe it.'

'It's true. But they moved him down when he refused to work.'

'But he's as thick as they come,' I said.

David shook his head. 'Don't you believe it. Jago's got a great deal of intelligence. It's just that he doesn't use it.'

'Talking about intelligence,' said Bob, getting to his feet, 'I think it would be wise if we bought some more coffee. Before Joe decides to throw us out too.'

I wasn't convinced. I looked at Erica. 'Don't tell me you believe all this.'

She looked at me with a curious expression in her eyes. 'As a matter of fact, I do. But what I can't understand is: why are you so antagonistic towards him? He can be fun at times.'

'I'll tell you why. Because he's a brute. And I don't care what anybody says, I can't stand him.'

That was my final word. Nobody was going to make me change it.

Chapter 5

Sunlight streamed through the windows the following morning as I awoke, lancing through a gap in the curtains, spotlighting the specks of dust which hovered in the still air. I sat up and pulling aside the curtains, looked out. The clouds had gone completely and the wind which had blasted in from the sea was now just a gentle breeze, stirring the branches of the budding tree outside. For a moment, though I knew deep down that something unusual had happened, I couldn't remember what it was. Then the memory came flooding back, scouring a deep hole inside me.

I remembered too that I hadn't heard my father arrive home the previous evening, even though I recalled glancing at the bright red digits of my bedside clock-radio just after midnight before I fell into a heavy slumber. But he was home now. I could hear him moving about downstairs from where the smell of fresh coffee and sizzling bacon wafted up. I slipped out of bed and slid into my slippers.

At that moment, he called up the stairs. 'Dianne. It's half-past eight. Breakfast's ready.'

Throwing on a dressing gown, I made my way to the kitchen. Dad had tied an apron round his waist and was in the act of ladling a fried egg on to a plate on which two rashers of bacon kept company with a slice of fried bread.

'Thought you had netball today. Lazy devil.'

I poked a tongue at him. 'I have. And what about you? You're normally at work by now.'

'It's all right. I've arranged for Roger Thompson to look after the fort for half an hour.' He glanced at his watch. 'Though I'd better step on it, I suppose. It wouldn't be fair to leave him in charge for too long.'

Roger wouldn't mind, I thought. Though he was only twenty-two, he was brimming with confidence, and I could imagine him jumping at the opportunity of looking after the supermarket all on his own.

'Where are you playing today?' he went on.

'Fairfield Comp. Away.'

Fairfield Comprehensive School was in the next town, about twenty miles inland.

Dad nodded and put his hand into his wallet. 'You'd better get yourself something for lunch then . . .' He slipped two pound notes across the table, and then added a further five pounds. 'I suppose you'd better have your pocket money now . . . before I forget . . .'

He always said the same thing; except that he never forgot.

'I don't need anything for lunch,' I said, pushing the two pounds towards him. 'We always have a meal in the school canteen.'

'Never mind. You might want to buy something.'

'But I won't,' I insisted, knowing very well that he was trying to compensate for my mother being in hospital. He wouldn't listen and I ended up putting the whole seven pounds into my purse and making a mental note to put some of it towards a new coat I'd been planning to buy.

He stood up and put on his jacket. 'I'll be home at six. How about visiting your mother this evening?' When I hesitated, he added, 'I think you should. I know she'll want to see you.'

'All right!' I agreed, trying to hide my apprehension. I'd heard some pretty scarey tales about mental hospitals.

'Good. I'll pick you up here, just after six. Visiting hours are until eight so we should have plenty of time.'

After he'd gone, I sat there sipping my coffee until I realised with a start that I'd have to hurry or I'd miss the coach which left school at half-past nine.

I met Erica half-way down the hill. She was about a hundred yards ahead of me, and when I yelled, she turned and waited.

'Hi,' she said as I got near. 'How's your mother?'

I shrugged my shoulders. 'All right, I suppose. Dad didn't phone this morning.'

She gave me an encouraging smile. 'Not to worry. I'm sure she'll be better soon.'

I wish I could have been so sure, I thought. It was all right for Erica to sound so confident, and I couldn't help wondering how she would feel if it were her mother. Then, as we reached the school, the coach in sight now outside the gates, I grabbed her arm.

'Look, Erica. About my mother. You won't tell anybody, will you? About her being in a mental hospital.'

'Oh, Dianne. Aren't you making a mountain out of a molehill? People can be very understanding, you know.'

I shook my head. 'I'd rather they didn't know. Please – please promise you won't say anything . . .'

'Of course I promise, silly. Now stop worrying.'

We reached the coach and, climbing aboard, discovered that they'd all been waiting for us. And Miss Ware was not amused!

I couldn't concentrate that morning, and I played a really grotty game. Miss Ware glared at me from the sidelines whenever I fumbled my footwork and even Erica gave a cry of exasperation when I missed an easy goal. And of course, when Fairfield won twenty-five goals to twenty, I wasn't the most popular girl in the team. Though it was only Sharon Pearson who made any comment. Dressed in her PE kit and devoid of make-up, she didn't appear as old as she had the previous evening when she'd been ordered out of the cafe with Jago. But the contemptuous look was still there.

'What did you think you were playing?' she

demanded as we jostled breathlessly into the changing room. 'Ludo? If it hadn't been for you, we'd have won that game.'

I felt myself go red. 'I'm sorry . . . I'm just off form, that's all.'

'Huh! That's all!' Sharon wasn't going to let me off the hook so easily. 'What if we lose the end-of-term tournament – just because you're off form?'

Erica came to my defence. 'Leave her alone, will you? You weren't so hot yourself.'

'What do you mean?'

Erica went up to her, thrusting her face forward so that it was almost touching Sharon's. 'What I say. You weren't much good at goal attack, were you? You missed some pretty easy goals yourself.'

'That was because of her.'

'Oh, yes. Go on. Blame someone else.'

Everyone else stopped speaking and some of the Fairfield girls who were already in the showers poked their heads round in surprise. But then Miss Ware came in, sizing up the situation at once.

'You can stop that. Both of you!' she ordered in her firm but quiet voice. 'I'm not allowing anyone to let the school down . . . on or off the court.'

I thought Sharon was going to defy her, but her stare wavered and with a flick of the head, she flounced back to where she had left her clothes. But when she looked at me, there was hatred in her eyes and I knew that I'd made an enemy I'd have to be extremely wary of.

When I arrived home after the usual lunch of sausage, beans and chips, there was a large cardboard box in the kitchen, full of groceries and an attached note from my father asking me to unpack them. There was enough to last a month – mainly convenience foods which we'd need more than ever now. I packed them away in the cupboards and then went upstairs to tidy my room. By the time I'd finished, it was three-thirty and when, at last, I sat down to read the latest copy of my pop magazine I realised with a shock that it was almost twenty-four hours since my mother had been admitted to hospital. I couldn't believe it. I felt as though it was someone else's mother who had taken that overdose.

It was a horrible feeling and I had to shake myself to get rid of it. Arming myself with a mug of sweet coffee and a plate full of chocolate biscuits, I went to my bedroom, tucked myself under the duvet, and lost myself in my reading.

It worked. The next hour slipped past and soon it was time to get Dad's tea. I knew he wouldn't want much before going to the hospital – certainly not the casserole which was still languishing in the fridge – but a sandwich and perhaps some pastries would be acceptable.

He arrived home sooner than expected, having left the final hour's supervision to the ever-ambitious Roger, and grateful for the snack I'd prepared.

'Just the job,' he said, taking a bite of ham sandwich. 'And a cup of tea would go down fine.'

'It's coming,' I yelled from the kitchen. 'Won't be a minute.'

Then carrying the tray into the living room and placing it on a low table, I poured out two cups. He sipped his tea and glanced up.

'By the way, I phoned the hospital this afternoon. They want me to take some of your mother's clothes over . . .' He paused. 'I think I ought to warn you. It seems she isn't too good. So if you'd prefer to come another time . . .'

If I wanted the chance of getting out of doing something I'd been apprehensive about all day, this was it. Instead I shook my head.

'No. I'd prefer to go with you.' I almost said: and get it over with.

'Very well. If you're sure.' He glanced at his watch. 'And now I suppose we'd better get ready.'

It was quite dark when we set out. Dad talked incessantly throughout the journey, trying with what seemed to be a quiet desperation to make things appear as normal as possible. As though having a mother admitted into a psychiatric hospital was perfectly normal. I kept wondering what it would be like, and yet, in spite of those horrible tales, when we arrived I found it wasn't a bit like I'd been led to expect. It was situated pleasantly on the brow of a low hill overlooking a meandering river; reflected in the dark tranquil waters were the electric-blue street lights of a small village on the opposite side.

There was a deep rumble as we crossed the cattle grid that guarded the main entrance and the headlights of the car swept past neat lawns and flower beds packed with daffodils and narcissi. Here and there, clumps of yellow crocuses burst out of the frozen grass. As my father parked outside a stone-built building with the sign 'Administrative Block' printed in bold black letters on a white board, my anxiety grew and I almost decided to stay in the car.

But the panic faded and together we followed the signs to Jubilee Ward which took us along a labyrinth of corridors and eventually up a narrow green and brown tiled staircase to a heavy oak door. It was locked. Dad pressed a button and we heard the shrill peal of a bell, followed moments later by the rattle of a key in the lock. The door opened and a young nurse in a light blue uniform admitted us. My father told her who we were, and for a moment I thought I saw a glimmer of uncertainty in her eyes as she glanced towards me. Then she led us along a thickly carpeted corridor, its walls lined with paintings, to a small waiting room.

'If you'll wait here, Mr Barrett,' she said with a smile, 'I'll get your wife.'

The room was tastefully furnished with a small settee, two side chairs and a low table near the window. Along one wall was a music centre with a stack of records underneath. As we stood there, neither of us said much and when we did exchange a few words, we spoke in half-whispers. In the distance we could hear the tinkle of dishes and the subdued murmur of voices. Glancing at my father, I could see he was as uneasy as I was.

Presently, the door opened and the same nurse appeared. I was surprised when she spoke to me instead of my father.

'Sister wonders if she could see you for a moment,' she said.

I glanced at my father and he nodded. 'You can see your mother later.'

I followed the nurse down another corridor until we came to some double swing doors which led into a large lounge already filled with clusters of visitors seated in deep armchairs. At one end was a huge colour television. Sister's office was on the immediate left and Sister herself was a plump woman in her early forties with dark hair half hidden under a starched cap. Her uniform was dark blue, and everything about her was neat, from her white collar to her immaculate cuffs. She gave the impression of being an efficient nurse who wasn't going to stand any nonsense. Yet her smile was warm and genuine.

'Come in, dear.' With a wave of her hand, she invited me to sit in the chair opposite her desk. Then she glanced briefly at the file in front of her. 'Your name is Dianne I see. I'm Sister Davis.' She obviously wasn't going to waste time on formalities. 'I asked Nurse Samuel to bring you here because frankly I don't think your mother's well enough to see anyone at present — except for your father, of course. But now you are here, I thought you might like to ask about her. I'm sure the past few months haven't been easy for you.'

'No – no, they haven't!' I croaked as I tried hard to control my voice.

She nodded sympathetically. 'You realise, don't you, that your mother's been suffering from severe depression? And that it hasn't been very pleasant for her either? It would have been better if she'd been admitted earlier.' She leaned back in her swivel chair and toyed with her pen. 'But that can't be helped. What we must think about now is what we can do for her. Is there anything you'd like to know?'

I shrugged my shoulders. There were so many things I wanted to have explained, but I didn't know what to ask first.

'I suppose . . . I suppose I'd like to know why she's ill. She's changed so much lately, and I can't understand why. It's not as though she's got anything to worry about . . . anything real that is. I mean, Dad's got a good job – we're not poor or anything.'

Sister Davis smiled indulgently. 'It's got nothing to do with that. And I think you put your finger on it a minute ago when you mentioned the change in her. You're an intelligent girl, Dianne. I'm sure you've heard about the menopause.' When I nodded, she went on. 'That's what's happening to your mother right now. It's come early, I know, but it does happen prematurely to many women. Anyway, to put it simply, I suspect the changes inside your mother's body have caused this depression. I'm sure in the last couple of years you've often felt down in the dumps for no apparent reason yourself.'

'Yes I have.'

'It's the same with your mother – except that it's happening in reverse.'

'I see . . .' I said slowly. 'Does that mean she'll get better?'

The eyes behind the glasses became soft and gentle. 'The only honest answer I can give to that is: I don't know. After all, which of us has the gift of foresight? But I personally would be very much surprised if she didn't. I've seen many women come in – like your mother – in a terrible state, and in time, with the right treatment, and of course, plenty of love, patience and understanding from their families, they've left and never come back. Though . . .' She paused before continuing. 'I think I ought to warn you, it's likely to take some time.'

'I see . . . How long?'

'Months rather than weeks. But of course, no one can predict with any degree of accuracy. She could be out earlier than that. It depends on many things.'

She went on to explain what Dad and I could do to help, and she answered all my questions honestly and objectively. Her calm manner made me feel very much better.

After a while, there was a knock at the door and Nurse Samuel came in. 'Mr Barrett would like to see you for a few moments, Sister. If it's convenient.'

'Yes of course.' She turned to me. 'It would be wise if I saw your father alone, my dear. But don't forget. If you'd ever like to see me again, just ask one of the nurses.'

Dad was half-way into the office by this time and as I passed, he squeezed my arm. 'Won't be long,' he whispered.

As I waited in the corridor, I saw my mother for the first time. She was being led back to the ward, aided by another nurse, and as she passed, shuffling pathetically in her slippers, she gave no sign that she was aware of my presence.

As for myself, I couldn't go near her. I don't know what it was, but nothing could have induced me to go up and put my arms around her. And yet that was exactly what I wanted to do.

It was a quarter of an hour before my father emerged and I had never been so glad to see him. Though the nurses were kind and cheerful and the decor was more like that of an hotel than a hospital, the atmosphere was claustrophobic. As we returned to the car, I breathed in gulps of fresh air as though I'd been locked in a smoke-filled room.

My father said hardly a word on the way home, but as he pulled into the drive and switched off the engine, he said, without looking at me: 'Dianne, I think it would be better if you didn't visit your mother again – not for a few weeks, at least.'

I felt nothing but relief. Those few words had taken the awkward decision right out of my hands.

Chapter 6

The next week saw me settling into a steady routine, and to begin with we managed quite well, though it wasn't as easy as my father had envisaged. The house was cold and empty when I arrived home – even though the central heating had been timed to come on at three o'clock – and cooking the evening meal took longer than anticipated. That, in addition to having to do the ironing as soon as I managed to dry the washing, meant that it was late before I started my homework. Revision was an impossibility.

I must be honest; Erica came over and helped whenever she could find the time but, like me, she had her own work to cope with. The worst thing I had to endure was the loneliness. My father would either be working late or visiting my mother – after which he'd invariably call somewhere for a drink, while David, who had just had the results of his mock 'A' level examinations and hadn't done as well as he'd hoped, was even busier with his revision. Apart from going to and from school, I hardly saw him.

However, on the following Saturday, his mother invited me over for tea before going to the disco. But as the four of us sat down to a table laden with all kinds of food, I suddenly thought of my mother in that dreadful hospital – and I lost my appetite.

Mrs Lucas was watching me anxiously across the

table. 'Come on, Dianne. It's not like you to toy with your food. Don't tell me you're going down with a cold or something.'

'No, of course not,' I stammered and felt my face go red in my confusion. 'I was just thinking . . . that's all . . .'

Mrs Lucas smiled at me. 'Well, finish up your salad. There's a trifle to come, and some fruit cake as well.'

I had a mouthful of cold ham which I managed to gulp down. 'I couldn't eat all that, Mrs Lucas – I'm full up as it is.'

'Nonsense – a young girl like you . . .'

'Perhaps she's thinking of her figure, Mother.' Mr Lucas, who was sitting opposite, winked at me, his eyes twinkling with mischief. He was older than my father, David being the younger of two children, though his elder sister had left home to get married over three years ago. 'A young girl thinks more of her figure than of food. Doesn't she, Diane?'

Mrs Lucas frowned at him, though anyone could see she was just pretending to be annoyed. 'Now leave the girl alone, George. You're making her all embarrassed.' She turned to me. 'Don't you take any notice of his teasing, Dianne love. Just you eat up your tea and ignore him.'

David looked over and grinned. He was eating his meal as though he were a famine victim. But then, he had been playing for the school's first eleven that morning and must have been ravenous.

I liked being with David's parents. Though they were getting on in years, they were so easy going – especially Mr Lucas who was a real tease. And though their rooms weren't as expensively furnished as ours, nevertheless an atmosphere of happiness and contentment permeated the whole house. I really did envy him.

I told him so later when we were in his bedroom listening to some records on his music centre. One wall was taken up with a fitted wardrobe, the opposite one with shelves containing a library of books, while the music centre was squeezed between his bed and his writing desk.

David lounged on his bed while I commandeered the bean-bag and sat with my back to the radiator.

'I really do envy you,' I said, listening to the Carpenters singing 'Rainy Days and Mondays' and making me feel really moody and misty-eyed. 'They never seem to quarrel – not like mine . . .'

David laughed. 'Of course they quarrel. They don't do it while you're here, that's all.'

'I know everybody quarrels. But mine seem to quarrel all the time.'

'That's probably because your mother's ill.' He said it in a matter-of-fact way. 'When she's better, it will stop.'

He had the knack of putting his finger right on the very core of a problem. I thought back to when I first entered the comprehensive school. We were all happy then. And yet there didn't seem to be any particular time when things began to change. It seemed to happen gradually.

'I suppose you're right,' I admitted begrudgingly. 'But it doesn't make it any easier for me . . . or my father either. Honestly, I know it's a terrible thing to say, but I don't know how he's put up with her for the past few months. I mean, I can't stand to be in the same room with her for more than ten minutes when she's in one of her moods. She nags him all the time.'

Tears began to sting my eyes. 'Oh, what's wrong

with me? All I ever seem to do these days is cry. You'll be getting fed up with me if I'm not careful.'

'Rubbish,' he said and rolled off his bed.

'Your biorhythms are all wrong.' He rummaged about in a pile of cassettes. 'That's probably the trouble.'

'Biorhythms?' I wrinkled up my nose. 'What are biorhythms?'

'I'll show you.' He tossed one particular cassette over to me. 'I bought that this morning. It's a computer programme. It works out your personal chart.'

I read the instructions on the leaflet that came with the cassette.

'Fancy trying it out?' he asked.

I was intrigued. 'Why not? It won't do any harm, will it?'

He turned off the music centre and plugged his microcomputer into the electricity supply and portable television set. Then he fed the cassette into his tape recorder and switched it on.

'It's feeding the programme into the computer,' he explained. 'It shouldn't take long. Just a couple of minutes.'

He was right. Two or three minutes later, it was loaded and David punched in my date of birth. Almost immediately, some graphs appeared on the screen. They were indecipherable to me.

'Ah. That explains it,' he said mysteriously, pointing to the wavy lines.

'Explains what?'

'Why you're feeling so low. It isn't just the fact that your mother's illness has been getting you down. Your biorhythms are at their lowest ebb.'

He pointed first to the row of figures at the top of the

screen. 'This is today's date, and here – ' he traced his finger to where three lines had met at the bottom ' – these are your emotional, intellectual and physical graphs. See where they meet? Right at the bottom.'

'So?' I was sceptical. 'That's just a coincidence.'

'You don't have to believe me. Some people – important people – take these charts very seriously. Just wait and see how you feel in a fortnight's time.' He pointed again to the top of the screen where this time the curves all met at the top. 'You'll be on your best form then.'

'If you say so.' I wasn't really convinced, but hoped at the same time that he was right. Then I heard Mrs Lucas begin to wash up the dishes and I hurried down to the kitchen to help her.

Of course Mrs Lucas objected and pointed out that I was a guest, but I wouldn't listen to her protests. We chatted about this and that, and then, as she put the last few cups away and thanked me, she paused and glanced at me thoughtfully.

'Look, Dianne!' she said. 'Please don't think I'm interfering, but don't let things get you down. I mean . . . I realise what it must be like for you at the moment, but many women at your mother's age go through a time like this. I know I did – though not as bad as your mother, of course.' She went on hastily. 'But it does pass – your mother will soon be out of hospital and things will be back to normal. Anyway, what I'm trying to say is this: if you ever want to talk about it, you know where to come, don't you? And if you ever need any help, you only have to ask.'

'Thanks, Mrs Lucas,' I said, wishing once more that my own mother could be just as understanding – instead of expecting to be helped all the time. 'I will.'

All the same, the fact that she knew my mother was in a mental hospital made me feel terrible.

The disco was held in a large hall at the rear of one of the largest hotels in town. We left David's at eight o'clock, calling at Erica's as arranged, to find that Bob was already there. I was glad; it would mean we would save time. I always enjoyed the Saturday night disco — it was the high spot of the week. The trouble was that it tended to get crowded so it was always wise to get there early. There was another reason too. It was restricted to the over-eighteens, presumably because of the bar, and at the door were usually one or two of several bouncers. Their job was to weed out anyone suspected of being under age. They were usually lenient when the place was fairly empty, but as it became crowded, so they were more watchful. One of them, Charlie, had thrown me out several times and I began to wonder if he had taken a dislike to me.

While the boys watched television, I joined Erica in her bedroom. She sat in front of the dressing table, applying another face. She glanced at me through the mirror.

'Don't you think you need some more make-up?' she asked, pouting her lips as she inspected her lipstick. She turned her head from side to side examining herself critically. 'What if Charlie's on the door? You know what he's like.'

I stood behind her, leaning over her shoulder, and looking at my reflection in the mirror. 'I thought I'd put enough on.'

She gave a snort of derision. 'Come off it. You can hardly see it.'

I looked at myself closely. Perhaps she's right, I

thought. But I didn't like too much make-up – and my parents certainly didn't – and I always kept to the absolute minimum.

'You could do with a lot more blusher,' she said. 'And some more lipstick wouldn't come amiss. Look. Sit down and let me put some on for you.'

Anxious to get into the disco, I reluctantly changed places with her. She would have done better if she'd put it on with a trowel; dark green eye-shadow and thick red lipstick. Goodness knows what I looked like.

'Sit still,' she ordered when I tried to protest. 'You'll have me smudging it if you're not careful.'

The threat was too much; I didn't move until she'd finished.

'Now look at yourself,' she said proudly.

She had certainly made me look older, but I didn't like what I saw. I decided to take it off as soon as I got in. If I got in.

'Right. Let's go.' She unhooked a coat from a hanger in her wardrobe. 'And let's hope Charlie's got a night off.'

David grinned when he saw me – until I hacked him playfully on the shins, and explained why I'd put on the disguise.

And of course, who should be at the entrance but Charlie.

Dressed incongruously in a black evening suit with satin lapels and sporting a white carnation in his button-hole, he looked like someone out of an American gangster film. And the bent nose and heavy-lidded eyes didn't help either. As we squeezed through the narrow entrance, I could feel my heart fluttering under the sophisticated black evening dress I'd put on for the occasion. But when his eyes, scanning every one of us, stopped as he looked at me, it almost jumped into my throat. But then he glanced away at others who were following and I breathed a sigh of relief.

The first thing I did was go into the cloakroom, wipe off the garish make-up – much to Erica's disgust – and put on some of my own. Lightly! Then we joined David and Bob, who not only had managed to commandeer one of the last empty tables, but had also bought the drinks. Lager for Erica and me; pints of bitter for themselves.

The room was longer than it was wide with a single row of tables along two sides. At one end, spanning the whole width was the bar with its gleaming mirrors and suspended bottles of spirits while in front were clusters of tables and chairs. Above was a balcony where you could sit and watch. At the other end was the disco itself with its banks of pulsating coloured lights. Around the walls were dimly illuminated lamps with red satin shades.

We sat for a while, absorbing the atmosphere and then David asked me to dance. The floor was crowded as he led me on and soon we were moving rhythmically to the heavy throb of the music. I loved that music. It seemed to ease all the tensions out of my body and all my worries became unimportant – meaningless, almost. I lived only for that moment. And when they played a slow number and David held me close, his arms around me, it was as though I were in another world.

I was enjoying myself so much that I was surprised at the way the evening flew. But then something happened which made me wish I hadn't gone to that disco.

David and Bob had gone to get some more drinks.

Leaving Erica to guard the table, I went to the cloakroom. It was as I was returning, squeezing through the crowd that thronged the entrance, that I felt someone grip my arm.

'Well! Well! If it isn't Dianne Barrett.' The voice was close to my ear and when I heard it, my stomach flipped over. It was Jago. He was dressed in tight blue jeans and a white t-shirt with the words 'University of California' printed in bold letters on it. His shoulders were wide, his arms thick and strong; his chest muscles bulged under the thin cotton. 'Fancy a dance, Dianne?'

It wasn't an invitation; more like an order as his grip tightened and he forced me on to the floor. As luck would have it, it was another slow number and Jago held me close.

I tried to push myself away. 'Do you mind? You're holding me too tight.'

He looked down, putting on a look of surprise as if he didn't believe me. 'Too tight? Don't tell me you're scared.'

'Scared? What's to be scared about?'

I twisted, trying to free myself from his grasp, but his body was hard, unrelenting. He shrugged his shoulders.

'Search me! You're the one who's acting like a kid.'

'I'm not!' I replied hotly. 'It's just— '

'Yes?'

'I don't want to be held so close – not by you anyway.'

'That's funny.' His slow supercilious grin made me furious. 'None of the other girls seem to object.'

I gave him a twisted smile. 'But I'm not one of your other girls, am I?'

However, he was impervious to my sarcasm. He just

66

laughed and holding me even tighter, moved deeper into the centre of the floor, making sure I couldn't get away.

The music ended and I thrust myself away, rushing for the cloakroom. I felt dirty, tainted by the sweat of his body and the sweet smell of whisky on his breath. I had to wash all trace of him off me.

I was drying my hands under the hot-air dryer when Sharon came in. She walked right up and in front of the other, prodded me with her fingers. Her nails jabbed into my flesh.

'Just you keep away from Jago,' she said coldly. 'Or else!'

I looked at her in amazement. 'What are you talking about?'

She stood with her hands on her hips, head held to one side, and a sneer on her lips. 'Don't come the innocent with me. You know what I'm talking about. I've just watched the way you were dancing with him. Couldn't get close enough, could you?'

I couldn't believe it was happening. 'You must be mad,' I said, pushing past her.

But she grabbed my arm and swung me round. Her eyes were hard. 'Oh no I'm not. I've noticed the way you've been looking at him. I'm not stupid.'

I was suddenly aware that the others in the cloakroom were listening with amusement.

'Look here, Sharon. Let's get one thing clear. As far as I'm concerned, you're welcome to Jago. I don't want anything to do with him – I don't even like him!'

But even as I said it, I knew it wasn't true. He certainly disturbed me. But deep down he excited me too.

Chapter 7

I loved Sunday mornings, lying in late, and snuggling comfortably under the bedclothes, listening to the radio until my father brought up a steaming mug of coffee. Even then I'd stay there, drowsing happily, thinking of what I'd do during the day, until at least half-past ten. But this morning, though it was only nine o'clock, I felt restless and the soporific feeling of contentment which usually enveloped me was absent. There was no sound in the house and I guessed that my father was having a much deserved lie-in too. Deciding that it was my turn to make the coffee, I put on my dressing gown, shuffled into my slippers and went downstairs.

The kitchen was cold, as were all the other rooms, so I switched on the electric fire and huddled in front of the glowing bars and waited for the percolator to bubble. I glanced idly through the pages of the *Sunday Mirror* which had been delivered earlier, and must, I realised, have been the sound that awakened me.

When the coffee was ready, I took it upstairs. My father was still asleep as I walked into his room. It was strange to see him alone in bed.

I shook his shoulder. 'Coffee!' I announced.

He groaned, turned on to his back, and then sat up, tousle-haired and bleary-eyed. 'Thanks, love.' He took the mug from my hand and blinked at the clock on the bedside cabinet. 'Is that all it is? Still, just as well. I've got a lot to do this morning.'

'Oh? What's the hurry?'

I sat at the bottom of the bed, cupping the coffee mug in my hands. I still felt cold.

'No hurry. It's just that one of the men at work has invited me over for tea this afternoon, which means I'll be visiting your mother early. Think you can manage to make tea for yourself?'

'Oh, Dad.' He still treated me like a child at times. 'Of course I can.'

'Fine.' He took another sip. 'Enjoy yourself at the disco last night?'

'Mm. It was great.' Then I remembered the episode with Jago and the subsequent encounter with Sharon. I stood up abruptly. 'Do you fancy some breakfast?'

He shook his head. 'Just a slice of toast I think.' Then as I left the room; 'I'll be down in a minute. Must put that joint in early.'

Erica had promised to come round to give me a hand with the cleaning . To my surprise, she arrived half an hour before I expected her.

'You're early,' I said. 'Thought you liked to lie in on a Sunday.'

'I do. But it's such a fantastic day, I just couldn't stay in bed. And anyway, I'm going out with Bob and his parents in their car this afternoon.'

Lucky you! I thought. It seemed everyone was going out except me. David had told me he had a lot of work to catch up with, and the essay I should have handed in to Miss Paige the previous Friday hadn't even been written.

'Are you all right?' she asked curiously, following me into the living room.

'Of course!' My reply was sharp, knowing that she was trying to find out more of what had happened the previous night. 'Why shouldn't I be?'

She got the message. 'No reason. I just wondered, that's all.'

Leaving Dad to prepare lunch, we did the hoovering and dusting in record time so that by half-past eleven we were trooping up to my room, armed with mugs of coffee and a plateful of assorted biscuits.

But I should have known she wasn't going to be content to forget the matter. As she burrowed into the bean-bag, she decided on a direct approach.

'You know David was jealous last night, don't you? You dancing with Jago, I mean.'

I gave a sigh of exasperation. 'Don't be so ridiculous. Why should he be?'

'Well . . . you were dancing pretty close.'

'I told you . . . last night. He made me . . . You don't think I liked it do you?'

'And all this false antagonism.'

'Oh Erica.' She was being deliberately infuriating. 'It isn't false – believe me it isn't! I loathe Jago – I can't stand him near me!'

She looked straight at me, a mixture of disbelief and amusement in her eyes. 'If you say so, but I think I ought to warn you. Jago fancies you – I can tell. Better not let Sharon find out . . .'

Now I was getting really angry. 'Look. Do you mind if we change the subject?'

'Of course not. What do you want to talk about?'

My mind went blank. I didn't know what I wanted to talk about. How about talking about you and Bob?'

'Me and Bob?'

'Yes. You and Bob.'

'What about me and Bob?'

'For goodness' sake, Erica. Stop repeating everything I say. Let's talk about you two for a change.'

Erica shrugged her shoulders. 'All right. What do you want to know?'

'Well . . .' I thought furiously, trying to think of something sensible to ask. 'Won't you miss him? When he goes to university?'

She pondered for a moment. 'Yes . . . I suppose I will.'

'You don't sound too sure.'

'Of course I'm sure!' She hesitated again. 'Though I must admit I'll probably find someone else.'

'Someone else? But don't you love him?'

'Naturally — at the moment. But I'm not stupid, Dianne. I know when he gets there, he'll find someone else. And then where will that leave me?'

'Oh . . . I see . . .' I hadn't thought of it like that before.

'After all, we must be realistic, Dianne. Though I love him now, it doesn't mean I'll always love him.'

'I'll always love David,' I said defensively.

'So you say now. But wait until he goes away and you meet someone else.'

I shook my head vigorously. 'I won't meet anyone else. I don't want anyone else.'

But she just laughed. In a nice gentle sympathetic way perhaps, but she still laughed. And it hurt to think that something so serious and important could be so amusing.

'Do you mind if we have Radio One on? I always listen to it on a Sunday morning.' Then seeing how upset I was, she went on. 'Do be sensible, Dianne. David will soon be going to college — meeting all sorts of new people. And in a couple of years so will you. Who can possibly tell what will happen then?'

She was right of course; and I knew it. It was just that I didn't want to accept it. I felt so secure when I was with David and that was something I wanted more than anything in the whole world. The thought that it might end made me feel sad.

Suddenly the midday time signal went and Erica stumbled to her feet. 'I'll have to go,' she said, gulping down the remainder of her coffee. 'Mum said dinner would be ready by half-past. And I don't want to keep Bob's parents waiting.'

After she'd gone, I felt ill at ease, disturbed by our conversation and the realisation that you couldn't be sure of anyone. Or anything. The feeling persisted throughout lunch. Later, as we were doing the washing up, Dad asked me what I was going to do with myself that afternoon.

I shrugged my shoulders and thought of the essay I had to write for Miss Paige. 'Some homework, I suppose,' I said without enthusiasm.

He sensed my thoughts. 'Don't fall behind with your work,' he warned. 'You don't want to fail your 'O' levels, do you?'

He went off to visit my mother, leaving me alone. I went to my bedroom and re-read the essay title. 'Hamlet is a typical tragic hero. Discuss, taking into consideration his character, his background, and the eventual outcome of his actions.'

Great! Now I knew what I had to do!

Normally, I like Shakespeare but all I could think of was the final scene with all that carnage. It depressed me so much I just didn't want to write about it, and though I tried hard to concentrate, forcing myself to write sentence after sentence, I just couldn't settle down. I was restless. I kept gazing out of the window, getting more and more despondent with every minute that passed.

In the end, I threw down my pen and sat on the window ledge. The sun was shining on a calm sequinned sea, its rays dancing on the surface, making it shimmer and sparkle in the cold spring air. It made me long to go there. A sudden flash – a sharp stabbing light from the edge of town – attracted my attention. I glanced and saw that it came from a bus trundling up the hill. I knew that it would wind through the estate and wait for ten minutes or so at the roundabout that served as a terminus. Then it would begin its journey back to town.

I made up my mind at once. Without bothering to change out of my jeans and woollen jumper, I put on my thickest jacket and hurried out of the house. Though the terminus was half a mile away, I arrived there only minutes after the bus. I made my way along narrow alleyways, down side streets past sleepy cul-de-sacs, until eventually I came out on to the main road.

The bus driver activated the automatic door as I approached and grinned as I mounted the steps. 'Off to meet your boyfriend, love?' he asked cheerfully.

I smiled coyly back. No such luck, I thought. David had told me the previous night that he wouldn't be able to spare the time to come out again until the following Friday. And then for only a couple of hours. I wished that I could be as dedicated as he was.

I paid for my ticket and sat at the rear of the bus, basking in the warm sunlight, though I knew that the gentle breeze still possessed the cold breath of winter. A few minutes later, the driver started the engine and the bus bowled down the hill far faster than it had come up, and soon it reached the covered bus station. As I got off, he gave me a wink.

'Don't keep him waiting, love,' he said.

I ambled along the promenade. The tide was in, and the waves crashed against the outcrops of rocks, black and threatening, sending showers of spray through the air. I loved watching the waves; they had a majesty and power all of their own, and they both thrilled and frightened me. But the soft breeze was still cold and in the end I took refuge in one of the painted wooden shelters that were placed at intervals along the wide pavement. Even there I wasn't safe from the wind. It gusted into the shelter, scattering scraps of paper in its wake and sending little dust-devils of fine sand dancing across the floor.

It was still better than being at home though; at least the fresh air made my head much clearer. At last, I felt ready to leave. The sun was low and I was chilled to the bone.

I glanced at my watch. The bus left in fifteen minutes and if I rushed I'd catch it. I hurried along the promenade when to my surprise and relief I saw my father's car approaching on the other side of the road. I crossed to the edge of the pavement and waved.

But he didn't even see me. He was too busy talking to the woman who was sitting at his side. She was fair-haired, pretty and much younger than himself and he was much too engrossed to notice me.

Ridiculously, I called out after him and started to run. As I did so, my foot slipped on the kerb and I fell heavily to the ground. There was a sharp pain in my ankle, a searing pain that made tears come to my eyes. I sat up and nursed my leg with both hands. Only half-aware, I heard a motorcycle come to halt a few yards away, its brakes squealing. Then someone ran over and strong arms lifted me off the road and carried me to a bench.

'You all right?'

I would have recognised that gruff voice anywhere, even if its owner hadn't raised the visor of his crash helmet. Jago Brown!

'Yes, thanks.' I bit my lip to stop myself crying as I put my foot to the ground and a pain stabbed right up my leg.

'Don't look like it to me. What you want to go and do a thing like that for?'

In spite of the pain – or perhaps because of it – I lost my temper. 'I didn't do it on purpose, did I?'

His head jerked back. 'Sorry – I didn't mean it.'

'What a stupid thing to say!'

He grinned foolishly. 'Yeah . . . suppose it was. What I meant was . . .'

'For goodness' sake, Jago.' The pain was making me feel giddy and sick. 'Does it matter what you meant?'

He had taken my shoe off and already my ankle was beginning to swell.

'What I meant was,' he said slowly, deliberately, determined to have his say, 'how did it happen?'

'I don't know. I started to run and twisted my ankle.'

He peeled down my sock and shook his head. 'You're not going to be able to walk home on that,' he said. 'Come on. I'll give you a lift on me bike.'

Me have a lift on Jago's bike? No way. I had my reputation to think of.

'Thank you very much,' I replied haughtily. 'But I'll manage on my own.'

I could tell he was offended. 'Be like that if you want to. Only tell me one thing. Why don't you like me? What have I ever done to you?'

There was no aggression in his voice and the directness of his question shook me.

'All I did was offer to help you,' he continued. 'Of course, if you're too proud to be seen with me . . .'

The truth struck home and immediately I was ashamed of myself.

'I'm sorry, Jago. It's just . . . it's just that it hurts so much,' I lied.

'OK then!' he said. 'Let's start again. Shall I give you a lift home?'

I nodded meekly. 'Yes, please.'

He helped me over to his motorcycle on the back seat of which was strapped a spare helmet which he handed me. I managed somehow to hop on to the seat.

'Now put your arms round me tight – that's it – and put your feet on them bars down there. And not to worry; I won't go too fast!'

It was just as well he kept his promise because I couldn't even rest my injured foot lightly. I had to keep it suspended in mid air until we reached home. And by then my thigh muscle ached like mad. Clinging to his shoulder, I limped to the front door.

'You all right now?' he asked, and when I nodded, said, 'Right. See you around then.'

Only when he got to his motorcycle did I call to him. 'Jago – thanks – thanks for the lift!'

He grinned and waved. 'That's all right. For a girl like you – any time.'

Then he rode off with a squeal of burning tyres and, banking to the left, disappeared from view. I opened the door and hobbled in. Perhaps Erica was right, I decided. Underneath that rough veneer of aggression and contempt, Jago wasn't such a bad guy after all.

Chapter 8

I was watching television when my father arrived home that night, trying to take my mind off my throbbing ankle without much success. In spite of having immersed it earlier in cold water until my toes were numb, pains still jabbed through it whenever I moved.

'What's happened to you then?' he asked, nodding at my foot which I'd wrapped tightly with a crepe bandage.

'I got this running after you this afternoon,' I replied, not without a trace of rancour.

His brow puckered. 'I don't understand.'

'You passed me this afternoon, when I was walking along the prom. There was I, waving like a real wally, and you didn't even see me.'

'Funny. I don't remember that.'

'I'm not surprised. You were too busy talking to that woman next to you.'

'Woman?' There was a slight pause. 'Oh, you must mean Liz — Liz Sinclair — she works at the store. She was at the hospital visiting an aunt or someone, so I gave her a lift home.'

He didn't look at me as he spoke, and I didn't point out that he'd been travelling in the opposite direction.

'Anyhow,' he went on briskly, 'how did you manage to get home?'

'A friend brought me.'

He went into the kitchen and filled a kettle. 'What friend? David?'

'No. Just a friend. He gave me a lift on his motorbike.'

He returned to the living room and frowned.

'I didn't know any of your friends had motorbikes.'

'Well . . .' I paused for a moment not sure whether I should tell him everything. 'He isn't really a friend. More of an acquaintance really.'

But my initial reluctance had made him suspicious. 'What's his name? This fella with a motorbike?'

I'd never lied to my father. 'Jago – Jago Brown,' I said lightly, 'but that's not his real name.'

He didn't give me a chance to finish. 'Big lout? Dark greasy hair? Looks at you as though you're dirt?'

I had to admit he'd described Jago accurately. 'Yes. That's him.'

He took a deep breath and his lips went tight. 'You can keep away from him.'

'But Dad. He only gave me a lift home.'

'I don't care. He's trouble. Only the other day he was caught shoplifting in the store – gave me a mouthful of cheek. He was lucky to get away with just a ticking off.' He shook his head. 'I don't want to see you with him – ever. Do you understand? Ever!'

When my father spoke like that, I knew it wasn't wise to argue. So I just mumbled a promise. And though it was a ridiculous vow to make, at the time I had every intention of keeping it.

The next morning, the swelling had gone down slightly so despite my father's protests, I insisted on going to school. Eventually, I compromised by letting him drive me, even allowing him to take me right into the school yard. Fortunately, we picked up Erica on the way so that she was able to help me as I limped up the steps into the building itself.

The first person I met was Miss Ware. She was dressed again in her grey track suit and I couldn't help wondering if she even went to bed in it.

'Don't tell me you've twisted your ankle,' she exclaimed, a look of horror on her face. 'Don't you realise that the area tournament is in a fortnight's time? Look – you'd better come to my changing room and let me have a look at that foot. Erica, give her a hand.'

She rushed ahead of us, bouncing along the corridor towards the gymnasium, her close-cropped hair fitting her head like a cap. Erica and I followed slowly. Miss Ware's personal changing room was barely six feet square, with a shower in one corner, and a heap of hockey sticks in another. It smelled of leather and old socks.

She nodded to a chair. 'Sit down there and take your shoe and sock off.'

She examined my foot, making me wince. 'Have you had it X-rayed yet? No? Then I think you should. Better go along to your family doctor right now . . . It's all right; I'll square it with your form tutor. But it's vitally important that you're fit for that match, Dianne. The team's playing well at the moment and I'm sure you wouldn't want to let us down.'

She arranged for Erica to come with me to Dr Richardson's surgery which fortunately was just a few hundred yards up the road. It was a large private house with the surgery built as an annexe which could be approached from a side road.

'I'll be all right now,' I told Erica as I waited in the queue to see the receptionist. 'Better get back. You don't want to go missing lessons.'

'Are you sure?'

'Of course I'm sure. I'll be all right.' I delved into my brief-case. 'Do me a favour though. Give this to Miss Paige.' I handed her my essay which I'd managed to scribble down just before going to sleep. 'Only keep your fingers crossed. I don't think she's going to be very complimentary about it.'

I had to wait until all the other patients with appointments had been seen before the receptionist finally told me I could go in. By that time, it was almost a quarter-past eleven. Dr Richardson was sitting in his chair holding my file in his hand. He glanced at it as he motioned with a wave of his hand to a chair.

'Now then, Dianne. What can I do for you?'

I told him about my foot.

'Good! Good!' He was a bald-headed man in his early fifties with bright piercing eyes that always seemed to be laughing. He rubbed his hands together as he came round the table. 'Let's have a look at it, shall we?' He went down on to his knees.

After an examination that took just a few minutes, he got to his feet and shook his head. 'You don't appear to have broken anything. But it's just as well to be sure.' He returned to his desk, took out a form and began to write on it. 'Take this to the X-ray department at the hospital and get your father to phone me in a couple of days. I should have the result by then. In the meantime, go home and put your feet up. Give that foot as much rest as you can. As a matter of fact, I think you should take the week off school.'

The hospital was too far away to walk – at least not with an aching foot – so I went over to my father's supermarket.

The first person I saw as I entered the swing doors of

80

the supermarket, its long plate glass windows festooned with brightly coloured posters advertising special bargains, was the woman I'd seen in my father's car. Dressed in a navy slim-line skirt and bright red blazer, she was talking to one of the assistants stacking the shelves. Her shoulder-length fair hair gleamed in the harsh strip lighting. On her lapel was a rectangular white badge announcing her name: Mrs Elizabeth Sinclair. So she was a supervisor.

I hobbled up to her, told her who I was, and asked if it were possible to see my father.

'Oh! So you're Dianne!' she exclaimed, suddenly interested and concerned. When she smiled, she revealed glistening white teeth and looked ever prettier than I'd first thought. She glanced down at my foot. 'I suppose you've come because of that. He was telling me about it this morning.'

There was a plastic-backed chair near the exit. She brought it over. 'If you sit here for a moment, I'll get Derek . . . your father.'

I felt foolish sitting in a near-deserted supermarket on a cold Monday morning while passing assistants and the occasional shopper glanced curiously in my direction. But soon my father was striding towards me, between avenues of shelves.

'Don't tell me. They sent you home.'

'No. Dr Richardson wants me to have an X-ray.'

'I see!' He scratched his head. 'Well, we'll have to see about getting you there, won't we? Just hold on a second. I'll just fix it so that Roger can look after things here.'

No problem there, I thought.

He was soon back. 'Let's get you to that hospital then.' Supporting my arm, he helped me hop and limp to the rear of the shop where his car was parked. Mrs Sinclair was waiting for us. She'd already opened the doors.

'Hope you'll be better soon,' she said with an encouraging smile as she helped me slide painfully on to the passenger seat.

She waited there until we drove away, giving me a cheerful wave. Though I'd only just met her, in a strange way I liked her.

For a change, luck was on my side. There was only one other patient in the waiting room – a little boy with his arm in a sling – but even so it took a whole hour before I'd gone through the whole process. Then, to my surprise, the doctor in charge of the Radiology Department came out and told my father that there were no broken bones and that all I needed was rest. I'd thought we'd have to wait several anxious days for the result.

So my father drove me home, sat me on a chair in front of the television and told me that on no account was I to do any work.

'You heard what that doctor said. Keep your foot up and take it easy.'

But I couldn't possibly do that, I realised. I couldn't leave everything to him when he arrived home from work. And I resolved at least to do something to help during that week – even if it was only preparing the vegetables for the evening meal.

And so began one of the most boring weeks of my life. The first couple of days were great. No school. Just sitting down all day watching television or reading magazines.

But then the novelty began to wear off – especially when I hardly saw anyone all day. David was busy revising for his practical examinations which were now just weeks away, so that he could only make fleeting visits, while Dad went to visit my mother almost every night after work. Erica came over once or twice and we tried revising together but though it was a great success as far as getting together was concerned, as a method of swotting for our 'O' levels, it was a dead loss. All we did was gossip, so that we had to agree in the end that perhaps it would be wiser to work on our own.

Of course, I had to copy up all the notes that had been given to the class during the day. Erica called round every evening to lend me her books, but since she needed them herself the next day, I had to do all the writing up during that evening. It was ridiculous really; I was wasting time during the day and writing furiously every evening when all the best television programmes were on.

Unfortunately, I found it increasingly difficult to settle down. I kept worrying about the amount of homework I had to do – not to mention revising two years' work. The more I worried the more insurmountable the problem seemed to get; and the greater it mushroomed in my mind, the more reluctant I was to begin tackling it. It was a vicious circle from which there was no escape.

And the way the housework was mounting up made me anxious too. For the first time I realised just how much my mother did about the house.

But Mrs Judd was great. She used to come in every day or two to enquire after my mother and on two occasions she had accompanied my father to the hospital.

She insisted on taking our washing when she

discovered that I'd wrenched my foot, and when she returned it, all neatly ironed, she brought in a large casserole dish containing Chicken Supreme. It was delicious and we both helped ourselves to an additional portion.

'Better take the dish back to Mrs Judd,' my father said next morning. It was the Friday after the accident and my ankle was feeling much stronger. 'She made a point of asking for it to be returned today.'

So, having made a mental note, I decided to take it back later that morning.

Mrs Judd's house was a large detached dormer bungalow with long gardens to both front and rear and a drive that led to an integral garage. Along the side that divided it from our place was a wide flower bed and a path made of crazy paving which led to a large conservatory which had been built on to the back wall of the bungalow and faced out on to the garden.

I opened the wide gates and walked up the gravelled drive to the front door. I rang the bell and waited for several seconds. Though there was no reply, I knew that someone was in because I had seen Mrs Judd herself only minutes before feeding crusts to the birds. It was seeing her that made me remember what my father had asked me to do.

I rang the bell again, keeping my finger longer on the button this time. But still there was no reply. It was cold in the shadow of the bungalow so I decided to try the back door instead. As I walked along the path, I knew I was right. There was someone in. I could hear voices coming from a small open window at the side of the conservatory.

'I'll be honest with you,' said a voice which I recognised to be Mrs Judd's. 'I'm not at all surprised to find out he's been carrying on. I mean to say, it hasn't been easy for him the last few months.'

There was a conspiratorial quality about her tone that made me stop under the window and listen.

'I know,' said another woman's voice which I didn't recognise. 'But who would have thought it of him — he's such a nice man.'

'And he's got a good job — very responsible.'

'And there's his daughter . . .'

Warning bells began to ring at the back of my head. But still I listened.

'I know . . . I know . . .' Mrs Judd's voice had a sigh in it. 'And the woman's so much younger than he is.'

'Who did you say she was? I'm still trying to place her.'

'You must know her. Calls herself Liz — married that Barry Sinclair who has the garage down on Western Avenue.'

'Oh yes. I know — very attractive, blonde, thinks a lot of herself. But fancy him doing a thing like that — and with his wife in hospital too.'

Suddenly, I went cold. My stomach went into a tight knot and I had to put my hand to my lips to stop myself being sick. Now I knew who they were talking about.

My father!

Chapter 9

I turned and ran. I left the casserole dish on the front doorstep, rang the bell once more and rushed back to our house. I could hardly see where I was going. I stumbled blindly up the stairs, flung myself on to my bed, and cried. I went on crying until my chest actually ached and there was a stabbing pain in my throat. It wasn't true, I kept telling myself over and over again, as tears trickled uncontrollably down my cheeks. My father would never do such a thing. Never. He loved my mother. In spite of everything that had happened over the past few months, he would never be so cruel.

And yet I had seen him with that other woman. He had told me her name. I had met her – even liked her!

There were other things I remembered too. Things I hadn't paid much attention to at the time. Like that slight embarrassment when I told him that I'd seen him in the car. The times he came home late. But more important still, I remembered the words he'd spoken when I confessed that I felt I'd been responsible for my mother taking the overdose.

I could remember the words so clearly.

'No. It isn't your fault it happened,' he'd said. 'If there's anyone around here to blame, it's me.'

Those words went ringing round my head until it spun, and I cried and cried until there were no more tears left and my whole body was completely drained.

Suddenly, I sat up in bed. I had to tell him what Mrs Judd had said; there was no other way. But if he admitted that her suspicions were true, I didn't know what I was going to say. Or do!

But I knew I had to tell him. I just had to.

I went into the bathroom and washed my face; afterwards, as I gazed at my reflection in the mirror, I looked dreadful. There was no disguising the fact that I'd been crying. At that moment I heard Dad's car pull into the drive and a few seconds later, I heard his key in the lock. He walked into the living room, returned to the foot of the stairs and called up to me. I managed to croak a reply and then, with my whole body trembling, I went down. He looked round as I entered the living room and his smile faded.

'Hey. What's wrong?' he asked. 'You've been crying . . .'

I had worked out exactly what I was going to say, but now I was so choked up, I couldn't speak.

'Come on, Dianne. You can tell me – whatever it is.'

All I could do was shake my head in despair, blinking back the tears.

'Now look . . .' He held my shoulders and gave me a gentle shake. 'How can I help you if you won't even tell me what's wrong?'

But now that the time had come, I couldn't. I simply couldn't. I pushed myself away and clambered up the stairs to my bedroom as fast as I could. Later – much later – when I had eventually composed myself and Dad had called to say that dinner was ready, I went downstairs again. My heart felt like a solid lump of lead and my stomach was so screwed up there was no room for food. Dad kept glancing over, urging me to eat, an anxious expression in his eyes.

'I wish you'd tell me what's wrong,' he said at last. He hesitated with embarrassment. 'You're not . . .'

'What?' I asked bluntly, unable to keep the antagonism out of my voice.

'Well – you know – you and David . . .'

I looked at him in bewilderment. Then I realised what he was getting at. He wanted to know if I was pregnant!

'Of course not!' I snapped. 'What sort of girl do you take me for?'

'Then what is it?'

By this time, I was totally in control of myself. 'I'd rather not talk about it,' I replied haughtily. 'If you don't mind.'

I put into those last few words as much contempt and disgust as I could muster. Which left my father hurt and perplexed.

David phoned unexpectedly and asked if I'd like to join him at his place. I didn't wait to be asked twice. Without bothering to button up my coat, I hurried through the darkened streets hugging it to me. A cold evening mist, heavy with moisture, had billowed in from the sea, forming damp haloes round the street lights, and cloying everything with its humidity. I was chilled to the bone before I had reached half way, and as I rang the bell I was actually shivering.

Though I tried hard not to show it, he knew at once that something had upset me. Accepting his offer of a cup of coffee, I followed him into the kitchen. He put on the kettle and turned.

'Come on, then,' he said, spooning out the coffee. 'What's happened? Is your mother worse? Is that it?'

I was so ashamed at what I'd heard that I hadn't

intended to tell a living soul, but the temptation to share my problem was too much.

Deep down I desperately wanted someone to tell me I was worrying needlessly and as I told him what I'd discovered that afternoon, David listened patiently in silence.

'So, there it is,' I ended lamely, because my suspicions sounded so ludicrous now that I'd actually told someone. 'I don't know what to believe.'

He was silent for a few seconds before he spoke. 'If you're asking my honest opinion . . .'

'I am – honestly I am.'

'If you ask me, you're making a mountain out of a molehill.'

'But, David . . .'

'Hold on. Let's look at the facts for a moment. What exactly do you know for certain? First, you saw your father driving this woman in his car. Well – he's already given you an explanation about that. And secondly, you overheard a conversation which linked your father with the same woman . . .' He sounded so adult, increasing my sense of childishness, that I became annoyed.

'And he often stays out late,' I pointed out stubbornly.

'So what? So does my father.'

'I know, but . . .'

'But what?'

'Well . . .' Now I was dredging my mind for reasons. 'He sees this Liz Sinclair . . . every day . . .'

'Of course he does. They work together.'

'Doesn't that give them the opportunity?'

'Oh, Dianne!' There was a mixture of amusement and exasperation in his voice. 'You're impossible. My mother sees the milkman every day, but it doesn't signify anything. Besides,' he went on, 'has it occurred to you that Mrs Judd could be wrong? That, like you, she has seen your father out with this Liz Sinclair – and put two and two together to make twenty-two?'

A lump came to my throat. 'I suppose you could be right.'

'I know I'm right. If you ask me, too many people spend too much time gossiping about things that aren't their own business – and causing trouble in the process.'

David was always so down to earth and his logic so clear cut and convincing that it was often difficult to argue with him. I looked up as he handed me a mug of coffee.

'I've been stupid, haven't I?'

'Yeah. And because of it, you missed out on your dinner, didn't you? Bet you're hungry now.'

I smiled sheepishly. 'Yes – I am a bit . . .'

'Let's go down the chippy then, after you've drunk your coffee.'

Strangely, the night air didn't seem so cold now that David had banished all my doubts and worries. We walked hand in hand through a mist that was both mysterious and exciting, I feeling happy in the knowledge that my fears were groundless. We reached the small shopping precinct half way down the hill where David insisted, despite my protests, on lashing out his money on fish fritters and chips for two. Then, laughing and talking, we walked back to his place and spent the rest of the evening listening to some new tapes he'd bought the previous weekend.

Before I left Mrs Lucas brought up a tray of coffee and toasted sandwiches, determined that I should have.

something to eat – though it was David who wolfed them down.

I apologised to my father when I returned home that night. I didn't explain why I'd been so angry and upset, just that I hadn't been feeling so good – and without actually saying it in so many words, blaming it on my periods. He seemed very relieved and when I went to bed, I felt much happier and more at ease with myself.

The next morning I was actually ecstatic and got through my chores in record-quick time and since David was away most of the day playing soccer for the school, Erica and I spent the afternoon window shopping in town for some summer clothes.

'Oh, I wish I were working,' I sighed, gazing enviously at a window full of the latest fashions. 'Think of what I could buy if I was actually loaded with money.'

'I know . . .' Erica had a wistful expression on her face. 'I think I'll marry a rich man when I'm older. Someone who'll give me a couple of hundred pounds and tell me to go out and buy anything I want.' She thought for a moment. 'Or fix me up with a credit card. That would be much better . . .'

'Where are you going to find yourself a rich man around here?' I asked.

'You never know. I could meet some fella here on holiday, perhaps, whose father just happens to be a millionaire.'

'Huh!'

'Well, why not? Miracles do happen!'

'Not to me, they don't.' I nudged her with my elbow. 'Nor to you either.'

She shook her head and sighed. 'No. I suppose you're right. But it's nice to dream, isn't it?'

I couldn't help but agree with her, but my dreams — my dearest dreams — were nothing to do with clothes. I longed for my mother to be home and well again, and for everything to be right between the three of us.

My ankle started aching as we walked home so Erica suggested we should all meet at her place that evening. When we arrived, she'd prepared a simple buffet of sausage rolls, sandwiches and bowls of crisps and her father had been to the off-licence to buy a bottle of Sangria. David and Bob had come armed with cans of lager. We watched television and listened to some tapes and records. As I sat in the warmth of the lounge, looking at Erica and Bob fooling about as usual, trying to decide which tape to play next, and David so quiet and serious, I realised just how lucky I was to have such good friends.

But on Monday when I returned to school for the first time for over a week, things started to go wrong again. Miss Ware warned me in the corridor not to put too much pressure on my foot as the tournament was a week nearer and she wanted me fit — really fit — by then. And there was a near-nasty encounter with Sharon at break when I was literally saved by the bell as one of the masters came into the yard to ring it.

She and a few of her friends, finding me alone, had formed a circle and cornered me against a wall outside the upper school foyer. Mr Donaldson, breezing out from the warmth of the staff room, had with a teacher's quick understanding realised the threat they were posing.

'Sharon Pearson! Get to your next lesson,' he ordered. There had been a hiatus — a moment when it seemed as if she were about to defy him. 'You heard what I said. Get going.'

She gave a slow contemptuous stare. 'See you later, Dianne,' she said.

But the promise never materialised and I discovered that instead of going to her class, she had truanted when Jago appeared at the school gates on his motorcycle.

However, it was my encounter with Miss Paige which was the most distressing. She had stormed into the room in a most livid temper. We were just chatting quietly to each other, but she slammed the door behind her, marched to her table and thumped down her books.

'Will you be quiet!' she ordered. 'Why aren't your books out? You've less than two months before you 'O' levels and all you can do is talk.' She picked up a sheaf of papers and waved them at us. 'And if you think these essays are good enough, you can think again.'

She went round the room, handing back the papers and making adverse comments about almost all of them. She paused at my desk and looked down, her face stern and disapproving.

'I think you'd better see me after this lesson is over, miss.'

Oh, no! I groaned inwardly. This was becoming too much of a habit. I looked at the mark. D minus. The lowest mark I'd ever had for an English essay.

'Very well. Look this way.' She pulled her gown round her body. 'Take out your anthologies and turn to Wordsworth's "Michael".' There was a rustle of papers and a few murmurs. 'That will be enough of that. I said take your books out. Not talk.'

She was in one of her grim moods and the fact that I had to see her after class made me despondent. And when she asked me to read, I was more strung up than ever.

I stood up and started to read.

'Louder,' she commanded. 'I can hardly hear you.'

I started again, made a complete mess of it, and she made me read two whole pages before telling me to stop. She then called on several others and we spent the last ten minutes discussing what we'd read, with Miss Paige throwing a few well-aimed questions at anyone who didn't appear to be listening. I made sure that I *was* listening.

The final bell rang and there was an audible sigh of relief from the class. One or two actually closed their books.

'That bell is a signal for me,' she said acidly, and kept us waiting another two long minutes before dismissing us. I arranged to meet Erica outside and then walked up the aisle and stood in front of Miss Paige. I tried not to display my impatience as she went through the ritual of gathering up her books. Then she looked up.

'I suppose you know why I want to see you.' She didn't give me a chance to reply. 'That essay was the worst you've ever submitted. I was insulted – I mean it – insulted. And that mark – D minus – it should have been an E. Just how long did you spend over it?'

I shrugged my shoulders and glanced down, unable to meet her stare. 'About an hour. I did it late one night.'

She gave a muted exclamation. 'It showed. Very well. This is a final warning, Dianne. If your work doesn't improve in the very near future, I shall have no alternative but to talk to your father.' She paused for a moment and shook her head in exasperation. 'Very well. You may go.'

Erica was waiting in the cloakroom, sitting on the low bench above the wire rack that was meant for our shoes. She stood up as I approached.

'What did she want?' Erica asked.

'The usual. Wanted to know why my work had deteriorated.'

'Didn't you tell her?'

'Come off it, Erica. How could I? Would you have?'

'Perhaps not.' We walked down the corridor. 'But perhaps it would have helped if she did know about your mother.'

I shook my head stubbornly. 'No!'

'What if I told her?'

We were walking down the steps into the school yard. I spun round angrily. 'Don't you dare. I don't want anyone to know my mother's in that place. Do you hear? Anyone. If you do, I'll never speak to you again.'

I turned and rushed away. She had to run to catch up. 'I didn't say I would,' she pleaded. 'I only suggested.'

I stopped suddenly and turned. 'Look, Erica. It's ten-past four. I'm fed up of school as it is. So why don't we forget about it?'

My anger and contempt hurt her and it showed in her eyes. And knew that if I wasn't careful I would lose one of the best friends I'd ever had.

Chapter 10

However, Miss Paige's threat had its desired effect. As I glanced at my father over dinner that evening, I noticed how grey his face was and observed the deeply etched lines of strain on his forehead. I felt guilty. To have Miss Paige send for him, complaining of the deterioration in my work and adding to the burden he was carrying would have been unforgivable. So after he'd left to visit my mother, I resolved that I would work really hard on the next assignment – a comprehension exercise from a past 'O' level paper – which Miss Paige had set the previous week.

But first I decided to phone Erica.

'It's me. Dianne!' I explained when I heard her voice at the other end of the line. 'About this afternoon, when I blew my top – I'm sorry. I didn't mean to be so beastly.'

'Oh, Dianne.' Even over the phone, the warmth in her voice was evident. 'There's no need to apologise.'

'But there is. It was a terrible thing to do – and you hadn't done a thing to deserve it.'

'But you were upset. It was only natural . . .'

'That doesn't excuse it. So . . . I wanted you to know I'm sorry.'

She asked me if I was alone. 'Would you like me to come over and keep you company?'

'Well . . .' It would have been nice to have her over.

'I was going to do some work – and remember the last time we tried working together?'

She laughed. 'Perhaps you're right.'

We spoke for a few more minutes before ringing off. I was much happier now that I'd made my peace with Erica. I went to my room in a far better frame of mind and spent an hour and a half on the comprehension exercise. At the end, I knew that I'd done my very best and felt much more contented. I even did some Maths revision before my father returned with the news that my mother was very much better and that in a week or two, if she continued to make good progress, they might allow her home for a few days.

I threw my arms around his neck. 'Oh, Dad. I'm so glad!'

He smiled down at me and his eyes were moist. 'So am I, love. Who knows? Perhaps she'll be home for good sooner than we expect.'

The following week was the best I'd spent at school and at home for a long time. I worked harder and surprisingly got a lot of pleasure out of it, especially when Miss Paige complimented me on the comprehension exercise I'd submitted earlier in the week. I started playing netball again but when she noticed me limping as an occasional twinge stabbed through my ankle, Miss Ware refused to include me in the team for the Saturday morning match. The only thing that upset me – though I took great care not to show it – was the way Stacy Heatherington kept hanging about David.

But even that didn't really dampen the feeling of euphoria that almost made my heart burst with joy.

I spent Saturday morning getting the house ship-shape after a week of neglect, though since there were only the two of us and Mrs Judd had done the ironing again, there wasn't that much to do. I made myself an omelette for lunch and soon afterwards Erica arrived. She flung herself on to the settee.

'Lost again,' she said with a sigh. 'Miss Ware was furious.'

'Good!' I said with glad sarcasm. 'At least Sharon Pearson won't be able to blame me.'

'Oh her. It was her fault we lost.'

'Don't stop. Tell me more.'

Erica looked up in surprise. 'That girl really bugs you, doesn't she?'

'You can say that again. After that night at the disco, I mean – warning me to keep away from Jago. As if I'd want anything to do with him.'

'I don't know why you dislike him so much,' Erica went on. 'He's rather nice looking in a macho sort of way.'

'If you like that sort of thing.'

'And he is a bit of a scream.'

'Is he?'

'Come off it, Dianne. You know he is. In spite of his wild ways, he often has people in fits down at the youth club. And a lot of the girls like him. Even Mr Saunders does, if you ask me. I must admit, I find him rather exciting . . . in a funny sort of way. Sometimes he makes me feel all shivery . . .'

The last thing I was going to do was confess that he had begun to have that effect on me too. 'So what! Some people find snakes exciting – but I bet not many would spend an hour in a cage with a python.'

It was time, I decided, to change the subject. 'Fancy a coffee?'

She nodded and, following me into the kitchen,

talked incessantly and got in my way. We returned to the living room.

'Have you decided where we're going tonight?' I asked, bringing in the coffees and the biscuit barrel.

'I thought we were going to the Spring Fair. It opened last night.'

The fair came to our town twice a year. Once in the middle of March and again during September, and had been there at those times ever since I could remember. My father reckoned it had its roots in antiquity.

'It'll make a change from the disco, I suppose. Bit more expensive though.'

'Not necessarily . . .' Erica grinned as she took her coffee. 'Not if we get the guys to pay.'

'Oh, Erica. How can you suggest such a thing! You know they can't afford it. Neither of them has a Saturday job.'

'That's their fault,' she replied airily. 'But if they want the privilege of escorting two beautiful girls – ' she emphasised the word 'beautiful', though you could describe neither of us as that ' – then they should expect to pay.'

'Huh!' I knew she was provoking me. 'Who's the one who's always on about Women's Lib?'

'Me, of course!' She walked to the table and took another biscuit. 'But that doesn't mean I have to make the ultimate sacrifice and spend my own money. Not if Bob is stupid enough to spend his on me.'

I shook my head in disbelief. 'Honestly, Erica. You're impossible. If I thought for a moment that you mean what you say, I'd never speak to you again.'

'Of course I don't mean it, idiot,' she replied, her eyes twinkling. 'But it's a good idea, isn't it?'

We discussed where we should meet and decided it

should be at her place at eight o'clock that evening. Which was a fortunate decision, because about half an hour after she'd left, my father arrived home unexpectedly.

'I've just phoned the hospital,' he explained as he poured himself a coffee. 'They said we can take your mother out to tea this afternoon.'

I noticed the word 'we', and sensing an initial reluctance on my part, he went on quickly.

'It's all right. She's much better, not at all like she was when you last saw her. This means she's making good progress – I suppose it's the first step before they allow her home for the weekend I was telling you about.' He paused then went on. 'I think you ought to see her . . . I know she wants to see you.'

I nodded. 'Of course I will, Dad.'

I noticed the relief on his face as he went upstairs to change. 'Better put on something decent,' he called down. 'We'll take your mother somewhere really nice.'

So I changed out of my comfortable jeans and put on a dress instead.

We picked up my mother and drove into the country. I had to admit that she looked much better. She was still unsteady on her feet – though the shuffling walk had gone – and Dad held her arm as he led her to the car. She smiled when she saw me and gave me a kiss, but deep in her eyes was a sadness, a kind of indefinable fear born of insecurity.

'It's so strange being out,' she said, glancing round and giving my hand a squeeze. 'But it's nice being together again.'

We drove through bare tree-lined lanes where only the occasional hazel catkins gave a promise of spring, and after a while turned into a gravelled drive that led to a large hotel. We found a table in the bay of a wide window overlooking the countryside. Below us, at the edge of a vast sweep of lawn, a river looped slowly through the valley, while above it a series of low hills disappeared into a hazy distance. The sun, appearing briefly from behind the clouds, spotlighted the whole scene as though it were a picture.

As we ate our sandwiches, followed by scones and fresh cream, we carried on a strange stilted conversation, my father pandering to my mother, pouring out the tea and treating her like a child.

'I'll do that!' she insisted once, resentment flashing briefly in her eyes. But as she held the pot, her hand shook and I noticed that she didn't offer to do it a second time.

Eventually, my father glanced at his watch. 'Time we went!' he announced.

'Oh, no!' Tears appeared in my mother's eyes. 'Not yet, Derek.'

'They told me two hours, Sue – no more.'

'But I can't go back there. Not yet . . . please!'

My father shuffled uncomfortably. 'Tell you what. We'll go for a drive instead.'

Within an hour, to my mother's dismay, we were back at the hospital. I gave her a hug. 'Don't worry, Mum,' I croaked as a large lump filled my throat and tears welled in my eyes. 'You'll be home soon. Just you wait and see.'

But as I watched her go, clinging to my father's arm and glancing round to give me a final wave, I knew that it would be a long time before she was allowed home for good.

After driving me home so that I could change back into my jeans, my father dropped me off at Erica's.

Leaving my mother had upset me and as I rang the front door bell, I knew I would have to thrust her memory firmly behind me before I could even begin to enjoy myself.

They were all waiting for me. Erica grabbed her duffel coat and yelled to her mother that she wouldn't be late.

'Come on,' she said urgently. 'Before I get the "home by half-past ten" treatment.' And we all dashed out into the chill night air.

The fair was sited about half a mile away on a piece of common land next to the railway and skirted on two sides by a wide bend in the meandering river. We could see its multi-coloured lights from the hill and hear the strident blare of its music. I gripped David's arm excitedly and laughed up into his eyes. Then I remembered what Erica had said that afternoon and took out my purse.

'Hold on!' I said, thrusting three pounds into his hand. 'Dad asked me to give you this.'

'What's it for?' he asked, mystified.

'What do you think? It's my share of the rides.'

He shook his head. 'I can't take this.'

'Why not?'

'Because . . . because I can't . . .'

'That's no reason,' I said firmly. 'Let's be honest. You can't be that flush with money, can you. I mean, you're in the same position as me, having to depend on our parents for pocket money. I don't think it's fair for you to spend all yours on me.'

'But I like spending it on you,' he protested.

'I know. But the rides are going to cost the earth. This way we can have a fantastic time, and I won't have to embarrass you when it comes to my turn to pay.'

'Well . . .' he began hesitantly. 'If you're sure.'

'Yes, I am sure. Please David – take it!'

'All right. If you insist.' He looked down at me. 'But when I'm in the big time . . .'

I stood on the tips of my toes and kissed him softly on the lips. 'When you're in the big time,' I said, 'I'm going to take you for every penny you've got. Surely you realise now what a terrible gold-digger I am.'

He grinned down at me, his eyes shining in the moonlight. 'That's a date,' he said, and then added, 'Now how about doing that again? I liked it.'

I kissed him again and this time his arms tightened round my waist as he held me close. When he let me go, my lips were tingling and my heart was beating so loudly I felt sure he could hear it. It seemed as though time stood still. But then there was a shout from further along the road.

'Hey! What are you two doing? We'll never get there at this rate.'

It was Bob, butting in as usual where he wasn't wanted.

'Come on!' I said, gripping David's hand. 'Let's catch them up.'

The fairground was teeming with people. There were stalls on both sides of the narrow lane that led to the field and we had to jostle and fight our way through the crowd that funnelled into it.

David bought me a sailor hat with 'Kiss Me Quick' printed on the band, as well as a huge stick of candy floss.

'What shall we go on first?' he yelled, in order to be heard above the raucous din of the steam organ blasting out its old-fashioned tune.

'I don't know. What about the Rocket Ship?' I

pointed to the whirling capsules that zoomed up and down amid the excited screams of their occupants.

We ran to the edge of the circular wooden platform, dodging the puddles of water, and waited for the ride to end. Then we dashed for an empty capsule, managing to beat Erica and Bob by a hair's breadth. A hooter sounded and then we were airborne as David pulled on the joystick. Up we went, up into the air, and all around us I could see the bright lights of the side-shows and further away the dimmer blue lights of town.

A moment later, David thrust the joystick forward so that we went into a steep dive. As we did so, the spin became more pronounced; I was pushed against him and it seemed as though some unseen force was trying to thrust me into space. I grabbed hold of his jacket and screamed. Then we were up again and I was flushed and breathless.

As we got off, I saw Stacy Heatherington with Donald Dando, a lanky sixth former with straight hair and acne whom she'd lured into taking her to the fair. She waved and came towards us. But I pretended not to see her, and turning abruptly, dragged a bewildered David after me in the opposite direction.

We went on ride after ride until at last we had just over a pound left between us.

'How about some chips?' David suggested when we rejoined Bob and Erica. There was a mobile fish and chip van at the exit and the aroma made my mouth water. We stood impatiently in the queue for a while.

'Let's try the Chinese take-away,' I said when we didn't seem to be getting any nearer the serving hatch. 'We'll be ages here – and anyway, they give you larger portions in town.'

The others readily agreed. We thrust our way through the oncoming tide of visitors to the fair and then ambled along the old towpath, the way lit by the intermittent glimmer of light as the moon broke through the clouds. The take-away was on the promenade and perhaps because it was empty, we were given bigger portions than usual.

We strolled along the wide pavement, our hands pleasantly greasy from chips and spring rolls. Presently, we leaned against the railings that lined the sea front, gazing into the darkness and listening to the thunder of waves breaking upon the sand. But a sudden squally shower of rain sent us rushing to the entrance of one of the hotels on the opposite side of the road. We sheltered under its canopy, huddling against the wall; just by chance, I glanced into the restaurant.

What I saw made my heart stand still.

There, seated in a secluded recess, their faces revealed clearly by the light of a table lamp, were my father and Liz Sinclair. They were laughing. I saw my father lean over and take her hand in his. The meaningful looks they gave each other were unmistakable. At that moment, a waitress approached with a bill which my father paid.

Then, to my horror, they stood up and weaving through the cluster of tables, made their way to the entrance where we were sheltering.

Chapter 11

I felt so sick that I had to swallow hard. All I could do for a moment or two was stand there with my eyes shut, willing it not to be true. But when I looked again, they were still there walking to the exit. David had been talking to Erica and Bob and hadn't noticed my agitation. Somehow I had to get them away from that door before my father came out, so I did the first thing that came to mind — I just ran. I shouldered my way past them and dashed down the road. David shouted and then I heard them all come pounding after me in pursuit. I didn't stop until long after I had turned the corner and only when David caught up with me.

'Hey. What's wrong?' he asked, gripping my arm and bringing me to a halt.

I couldn't tell him — not when Erica and Bob came crowding anxiously round, puzzled by my behaviour. I just shook my head. 'I'm not feeling well,' I lied. 'I want to go home.'

I turned and began to walk quickly away. David kept up with me and eventually we left the other two far behind. He must have suspected that something had occurred to upset me, because only then did he grab my arm and make me stop.

'Come on, Dianne. What's up? Something happened back there. Was it something I said?'

I shook my head, blinking back the tears. 'No – it's nothing to do with you.'

'Then tell me. What is it?' When I didn't reply, he went on. 'Please tell me. How can I help you when I don't know what's wrong?'

I gulped hard as I tried to control my voice. 'Do you remember what I told you about my father? What I overheard Mrs Judd say? Well . . . I saw him with Liz Sinclair, only a few minutes ago, back there at the hotel.'

'Is that why you ran away?'

'Yes . . . they were holding hands . . . and . . . Oh, David! It's true after all!'

His eyes were serious and he didn't say anything for a moment or two. 'I see,' he said, biting his lip.

Something in the way he said it made me suspicious. I looked, saw his guarded expression and realised what it meant.

'You knew!' I said, drawing away. 'You've known all along – haven't you?'

It was more of an accusation than a question.

'No, I haven't.'

'Yes you have. You told me it was all my imagination, yet you knew it was true.'

He frowned. 'I did hear . . . but later . . . not then.'

Suddenly, the anger which had been lying just below the surface erupted.

'Why didn't you tell me?' I demanded.

'How could I, Dianne? Have a heart.'

I thought of all the others who must know. Erica and Bob. Their parents. Our neighbours. Everybody! And no one saying anything because they felt sorry for me.

'It was the least you could have done. You should

107

have warned me.'

I turned and ran up the hill with David still keeping pace with me.

'How could I? What would you have said if I had told you?'

I didn't answer him. There was nothing I could say.

'And anyhow, there's probably nothing to it.'

I stopped dead. 'Nothing to it? Don't be so stupid.' My voice was harsher, my tone more sarcastic and contemptuous than I'd intended it to be. 'If you'd seen them – holding each other's hands, smiling . . .' Words failed me. 'Oh, leave me alone, will you?'

I pushed him away and ran as fast as I could around the corner and into our street. When I reached the front door, I half expected him to be following me. But he was still at the corner. He stood there for a moment, then he turned and walked out of sight.

I closed the door behind me and leaned against it in the darkness of the hall. It was our first quarrel – our very first – and there was only one person to be blamed for it. My father!

It was at that moment that I really began to despise him. Not only for the way he was deceiving my mother, but also for causing the rift between me and David. For that, I vowed, I would never forgive him. Never.

I went immediately to bed. I couldn't be bothered even to make myself a cup of coffee though I was cold and shivering. I just threw myself on to my bed and cried. I was still awake two hours later when I heard my father let himself into the house. I hadn't undressed, but even so I slipped under the sheets knowing what would happen in the next few minutes. I was right. The door opened and he looked in.

I lay my head against the pillow and pretended to be

asleep. Only when the door had shut firmly did I sit up. Why hadn't I had the courage to confront him with what I knew? I asked myself. Why didn't I make him put a stop to it all? I didn't have to be told the answer, I had told myself: I just didn't have the courage.

I awoke next morning feeling muzzy and tired as though I hadn't closed my eyes all night. Dad was already downstairs, seated in the dining recess. He looked up from his breakfast as I walked into the kitchen.

'Hi. Do you want some breakfast?'

I couldn't bring myself to look at him. 'I'll get it myself,' I replied.

'No trouble. It's boiled eggs today.'

He got up and went to the fridge.

'I said I'll do it,' I snapped.

My father just frowned. 'All right. If you're sure . . .'

I was sure all right. I didn't want him doing anything for me.

It was a repetition of the day I'd overheard Mrs Judd talking — except this time I knew that the gossip was true. For the rest of the morning, Dad tried to make polite conversation but I just ignored him. In the end, he gave up the battle and we ate our lunch in utter silence.

'I'm going to see your mother,' he said as he cleared the table. 'Would you like to come?'

I didn't reply.

'I'm sure she'd like to see you again . . . like yesterday . . . she's better when you come . . .'

Still I didn't say anything.

He paused. 'I think you ought to come.'

Suddenly I couldn't take any more. I flung down the tea towel. 'For God's sake, Dad. Leave me alone, will you?'

I made for the door, but before I could reach it, he grabbed me by the arm and spun me round.

'Right. This has gone on long enough.' His jaw was firmly set and determined. 'You've ignored me all morning. I want to know what I've done.'

For a moment, I just glared back at him, and the words which had been whirling about in my mind all morning were now on my lips. My whole body was trembling, ready to blurt them out. But something stopped me.

'I said leave me alone. Can't you understand? Leave me alone.'

I tugged myself free, rushed upstairs, and locked myself in my room. He came up, knocked and pleaded with me. When I refused even to answer, he went downstairs. Eventually, he called up and said he was leaving. I heard the front door slam and a few moments later, his car drove away. I flung myself on to my bed and gave a sigh of sheer despair. I felt all my pent-up emotions surge around inside me, striving to get out, and yet there was a constriction round my chest which prevented them.

I forced myself to sit at my desk and tried desperately to get on with some work, but it was no good. Every few moments I'd look up and the same old thoughts would assail me, nagging at my mind until I wanted to scream.

In the end, I couldn't take any more. I put on a heavy coat, slung a scarf round my neck and left the house.

I found myself walking away from town; crossing the golf course which lay to the west and cutting through a ridge of sand dunes, I came out on a stretch of sand. The promenade was a good half mile away.

The March winds had died away completely, and now that April was approaching, the breeze which wafted off the waves was like a gentle feather that fanned my face. I liked looking at the sea, at the breakers that crashed on to the beach and rippled on the sand. They seemed to relax me, soothing away the tensions that not so long ago had made me want to scream. I sighed and shook my head. Where was it all going to end? I wondered.

Suddenly, I was aware of a motorcyclist riding along the hard sand towards me. The machine came to a halt a few yards away, its rear wheel skidding and scattering a shower of sand in my direction.

The rider was Jago.

'Sorry. Didn't mean to do that,' he said as I shielded my eyes.

My heart sank. I wanted to be alone. 'What do you want?' I asked ungraciously.

'Nothing. Just wondered if everything is all right, that's all.'

'Of course everything's all right.' I was immediately on the defensive, wondering if he too had heard about my father and Liz Sinclair. 'Why shouldn't it be?' Now I was being paranoiad!

He shrugged his shoulders. 'No reason. Just saw you all alone and thought I'd see if you were OK. That's all. Of course, I know when I'm not wanted.'

Now that I'd offended him, I thought of the previous week when he'd given me a lift home. 'Jago,' I called as he prepared to ride away, 'I'm sorry. I wasn't feeling my usual self, that's all.'

He grinned and wheeled his bike back. 'That's more like it. Thought for a moment you didn't want to be seen with me.'

'Don't be ridiculous. Why should you think that?'

'Because I'm me – Jago Brown. The guy who's always in trouble. Because – let's be honest – a girl like you wouldn't want to be seen dead with a guy like me.'

'That's stupid.'

'Sure?' He smiled when I nodded. 'Great. Now let's begin again. I'm Jago Brown – the guy everyone loves to hate, especially the fuzz.'

I had to laugh; he made even the truth sound funny.

He looked across at me. 'I like to see you laugh, Dianne. You're a pretty girl – but when you laugh, you're fantastic!'

He made me blush and all I could do was mumble something stupid.

'Right then. How about a spin on me bike?'

I hesitated for a moment and he went on.

'Now don't go saying "No" because then I'd really think you didn't want to be seen dead with me.'

Why shouldn't I? I wondered. Why should I worry what my father thought? What harm was there in it anyway?

'All right!' I said. 'I'd like that!'

He gave me the spare helmet and when I was seated behind him, he turned his head. 'Where do you fancy going?' he yelled, above the roar of the engine.

'I don't mind. Anywhere you like.'

'OK. Hold on tight.' Revving his machine, he pulled away and tore along the stretch of sand.

I clung to him, burying my head against his broad shoulders, shutting my eyes against the stinging grains of shingle. Then he drove up the slipway to the promenade and as we left town and started to wind up the road that led to the hills, I raised my head and felt the wind whip past my face, fanning my hair backwards. When he banked, I leaned with him, my body merging in motion with his own. Trees and hedges sped by, sunlight flashing between them, until about ten minutes later he pulled into a lay-by.

'Come and look at this.' He led me to a natural platform on the side of the hill. 'What do you think of it?'

The view was breath-taking. Hundreds of feet below us, the whole countryside was laid out like a map. Small fields and narrow lanes merged gradually with the town. I could see the river meandering like a steel-grey snake to the sea. I noticed the way the road and railway followed it to the town square. And I saw the golden sands curving like a scythe, cutting into a deep blue sea. It was fantastic.

'Do you know,' he said wistfully, 'I like coming up here. Makes me feel . . . makes me feel . . .' He struggled for the right word. '. . . Insignificant. That's it — insignificant.'

That touch of poetry was so unexpected, I glanced at him in surprise. And marvelled at the way I was learning something new about Jago almost every time I met him.

Chapter 12

The next morning the weather had changed; thick dark clouds, heavy with rain, scudded across the bleak sky, drenching the countryside with a steady downpour. I left the house, put up my umbrella and held it in front of me like a shield from the gusting wind. I had been thinking of David and since I had to admit that I couldn't blame my father entirely for our quarrel, it was up to me to sink my pride and apologise. But the fact that David hadn't been in touch made me apprehensive.

He wasn't waiting at his usual place so I glanced at my watch and saw that it was only eight forty. Perhaps he hadn't left home yet, I thought; perhaps I could meet him half way. Besides, it was better than waiting at that exposed spot and getting soaked to the skin. Already, my knee-length white socks were wringing wet.

But five minutes later, when I arrived at his house, there was still no sign of him. I stood in the rain, debating whether or not to call. It was ridiculous, but I was scared of meeting him – in case he wanted to have nothing more to do with me. Eventually, with my stomach twisting itself into knots, I walked up and rang the bell. I could tell somehow as it pealed out that the house was empty. I rang three times and receiving no answer, walked away. He had obviously left early and the fact that he hadn't been waiting for me at the corner of our road could mean only one thing.

He didn't want to see me again!

I wandered bleakly down the road, lost in my misery, and waited for a delivery van to pass before crossing. I hadn't noticed the large puddle at the side.

The van plunged into it and a sheet of dirty water cascaded on to me. It soaked my raincoat, my skirt, my slip – even my underwear was wet. I stood there speechless as water dripped into my shoes. I was so upset I could have cried.

There was no way I could go to school in that condition. So, feeling even more dejected than ever, I returned home, stripped off completely and immersed myself in a hot bath. I stayed home for the rest of the day, and by next morning I had a cold to end all colds. I felt wretched, especially when nobody – not even Erica – called or phoned to see how I was. I couldn't understand it; I hadn't quarrelled with Erica and I just couldn't understand why she should shun me. I felt so lonely and isolated, though with dark eyes and lank hair, and a nose so red in contrast with the rest of my face, having visitors was the last thing I wanted.

I had lost David now. So what was the use of even trying to look pretty.

In one way, however, having a cold was an advantage. It meant I had an excuse to keep away from my father. Whenever I heard his car pull into the drive, I'd leave the comfort of the fire and rushing to my bedroom, I'd bury myself under the bedclothes. Of course, he came up and asked me how I was, but all I'd do was answer in monosyllables. When he went out, I'd creep back down, switch on the television and spend the evening moping in front of it.

But on the Thursday evening, I felt much better. Moreover, I'd had enough. I just had to find out why Erica was keeping away; I'd done nothing to her.

So I picked up the phone and dialled her number.

Erica managed to sound surprised and peeved at the same time. 'Hey. Where have you been all week? I expected you around when I didn't turn up at school.'

'What do you mean?'

'I've been indisposed, as Miss Paige would say. Why haven't you been to see me?'

'Oh, no!' It hadn't occurred to me that Erica might

115

have been ill too. 'But I've been home all week as well . . .'

'You haven't . . . how strange. I had this terrible cough and I lost my voice. And of course Mum blamed going to the fair without a scarf. Well, she would, wouldn't she? Parents!'

'Oh, Erica. I'm sorry. Had I realised I'd have phoned before now. I thought . . . I thought you were annoyed with me after last Saturday.'

'Annoyed? Why should I have been? David explained that you were feeling ill.'

So he hadn't divulged the true reason for my behaviour. 'Er – have you seen David lately?' I asked.

'No, not since Sunday when he and Bob called round. But then I didn't expect to. Bob's been busy all week . . .' There was a pause. 'But hasn't David been to see you?'

'No . . . no he hasn't . . .'

'Oh . . . I see . . .' I could tell from her tone that she knew something I didn't. Fortunately, I didn't have to ask her what it was, because she went on. 'Look, Dianne. I know it's none of my business, but what exactly did happen between you two last Saturday? David didn't say much, but I could tell he was terribly upset.'

I gave a deep sigh. 'Oh, Erica. I've been such a fool. We had this quarrel. Well, it was me actually – I told him to go away – to leave me alone.'

'Ah!' She sounded as though a great mystery had been solved. 'Look. Tell me not to poke my nose where it's not wanted if you like, but why don't you phone him tonight? I'm sure he'll be only too pleased to hear from you.'

'Do you think so?'

'Like I said: I'm sure of it.'

'All right then. I will.'

'Great. I'll let you get on with it. By the way, I'm going in to school tomorrow. How about you?'

Suddenly, it seemed a good idea. 'Yes. I'll be there too.'

We arranged to meet and rang off. I replaced the receiver and picked it up again immediately, intending to phone David. But I didn't. I tried to make excuses, telling myself that David would be busy . . . that I didn't want to disturb him. But the reason was something quite different: I was just plain scared. I put down the phone.

I decided instead to be outside the sixth form common room before he arrived next morning. But as I turned the corner of the building, a shock awaited me. David was already there, talking to Stacy Heatherington. He had his back to me, but Stacy didn't. I saw her eyes flicker in my direction and she looked up at David and smiled.

'It was nice of you to ask me round last night,' she said in a voice that was extra loud for my benefit. 'I really did enjoy listening to your records. Perhaps you could come over my place some time. I've got stacks of LPs.'

'Yeah,' David replied. 'Not tonight, though.'

'That's all right. I understand if you've got too much work on.'

'Another time then . . .'

At that moment, Stacy glanced over his shoulder and put her hand to her lips, pretending to have seen me for the first time. David looked round, and when he saw me, he went red. He opened his mouth to say something and moved towards me. But I couldn't stay there; I just ran.

I arrived at the classroom just before Miss Paige, and I was so upset that I couldn't speak. Which made Erica so confused that wisely she didn't ask me what was wrong. I couldn't concentrate on my work and I was glad when, an hour and a half later, the bell rang for break. The last thing I wanted to do was meet David so instead of meeting Erica in our usual spot, I wandered to a bench at the side of the playing fields.

It was the worst place I could have chosen, because though I didn't know it at the time, Sharon Pearson had been looking for me all week. And she found me. It was the combined shadows of four girls that made me look up. My heart gave a quick flip. One of them was Sharon, and the look in her eyes told me to expect trouble.

She didn't waste words. 'I thought I told you to keep away from Jago,' she said bluntly.

I stood up. 'And I told you I wasn't interested in him.'

'Huh!' She stood with her hands on her hips, elbows out, her head thrust forward aggressively. 'Then how come you were with him all Sunday afternoon?'

This was ridiculous. 'I went for a spin on his bike because he asked me to. Do I have to ask your permission?'

Her eyes went cold. 'Jago's my fella — mine, do you hear?'

'Why?' I gave a maliciously sweet smile and pushed past her. 'Don't you trust us or something?'

'I wouldn't trust you further than I could throw you. After all . . . it runs in the family, doesn't it?'

Her words made me turn. 'What do you mean?'

Sharon returned my smile. 'What I say. Who'd trust a girl whose mother's in a looney bin, and her father's running after a woman young enough to be his daughter.'

I felt suddenly cold and yet there was a fury rising inside me that I knew I couldn't control. 'What did you say?'

'You heard. Like father, like daughter.'

That did it. I lunged out, caught her hair and spun her round. She fell to the ground. The other girls came towards me, threatening. But there was something in my expression that made them back away.

'Get up!' My teeth were clenched and I spat out the words. 'Get up and say that again.'

She rolled away and in an instant was on her feet. Her eyes were wary, but her lips were sneering.

'Your father's a randy old man.'

This time she was on her guard. When I struck out, she was ready. She gripped my arm and the next moment we were locked together, rolling on the grass, screaming and scratching each other, and kicking like a pair of wild animals.

I was dimly aware of the delighted howls of the others and then strong arms gripped me, jerking us apart. 'Stop it!' a voice was shouting. 'Stop it at once.'

It was Miss Paige. She stood between us while one of the masters held Sharon. Suddenly, as I watched, Sharon started to cry.

'I'm sorry, Miss Paige.' False tears were streaming down her face. 'She started it – I haven't done a thing.'

It was such a blatant lie that I gaped at her. But Miss Paige was not easily deceived. 'And you did nothing to provoke this incident, I suppose?'

'No, Miss!' She put on the performance of a lifetime. 'We were just walking . . . and she told me to keep away from Jago Brown . . .'

'That's a lie. It's not true!'

'Be quiet!' ordered Miss Paige. 'Both of you. We'll let the headmaster decide who's telling the truth.' She looked over my shoulder. 'David, take Dianne to the headmaster. Tell him I'll be along in a few minutes.'

Only then did I realise that it was David who was holding my arm. Oh, no! I moaned inwardly. Whatever would he think of me now?

Sharon saw the headmaster first, while I waited in the deputy head's room. I felt such a fool. I had fallen for Sharon's trap and now I was in real trouble. Presently Miss Paige came in and asked me to follow her. Mr Turnbull was seated behind his desk which was situated at an angle in the furthest corner of the long room. He leaned back in his chair and folded his hands over his stomach.

'Before I start I have to say this, Dianne Barrett. This is the first time you've been brought to me on a matter like this, and I am appalled . . .'

He paused and leaned forward. 'No . . . horrified is a better word.'

The room was silent for a few moments. In the distance I could hear the muted voice of a teacher shouting; a lorry passed along the road with a low growl.

'I'm waiting, Dianne. I've heard Sharon's explanation. Now I want to hear yours.'

I bit my lip, looking at the sombrely patterned carpet, and shook my head.

'Am I to assume that I should believe Sharon Pearson?'

'No, sir.'

'Then what she's told me isn't true.'

'That I attacked her? No, sir.'

'Yet her friends confirm her story.'

'They would, wouldn't they?' My words came out defiantly. 'I'm sorry, sir,' I added when I saw the disapproval in his eyes.

He rubbed his jaw and I felt it was to hide the grin that was lurking there. He glanced at Miss Paige.

'What's her work been like this term?'

There was a moment's hesitation. 'She started very well – very well indeed – but lately there's been a marked deterioration.'

'I see . . .' He turned back to me. 'Now come on, Dianne. Let's be sensible. What exactly happened today?'

I gave an inaudible sigh. 'I'm sorry, Mr Turnbull. I can't tell you.'

He breathed deeply and sat back in his chair. 'Very well. You leave me with no alternative. I shall send for your parents immediately. I am not prepared to accept this kind of behaviour from anyone – anyone.'

He dismissed me and ordered me back to my class. But my troubles were far from over. David was waiting outside and from the expression on his face, I had some explaining to do!

Chapter 13

'What on earth's got into you?' he demanded as soon as I'd closed the door behind me. 'That was a stupid thing to do.'

'Perhaps it was. What business is it of yours?'

I brushed past him but he followed me down the corridor. 'Come off it. You know very well it *is* my business. Honestly, I couldn't believe my eyes when I saw it was you. Why, Dianne? Why?'

'If I told you, would you believe me?' We came to the well at the foot of the stairs; my classroom was on the second floor. He caught my arm and held me back.

'Of course I'd believe you. Why shouldn't I?'

'Nobody else seems to.'

'Perhaps you should try explaining.'

'Explaining? Tell them that my mother's in a mental hospital? That my father's carrying on behind her back?'

David frowned. 'Is that what Sharon said?'

'That . . . among other things.'

'So she did provoke you. You should have told them.'

'Don't be stupid. I've told you before – I'm not going to wash my dirty linen in public.'

He shook his head. 'All right. There's no need to be so aggressive. I don't know what's come over you recently. You're not the same person.'

'Is that why you didn't call round last week?'

'Of course not. I was working.'

I spun round. 'Working? That's a good one. With Stacy Heatherington cooling your brow, I suppose.'

He had the grace to blush. 'She asked if she could borrow my John Lennon album, and . . .'

'And you asked her in.'

'What else could I do? I couldn't keep her waiting on the doorstep.'

'Of course not. You had to make things nice and cosy. And of course, this morning when she spoke to you . . . you were lapping it all up.'

A frown puckered his forehead and his lips went tight. 'You'd better go to your lesson,' he muttered. 'We'll talk about this when you're in a better mood.'

He made me see red. 'Who do you think you're talking to? I'll go when I'm ready – not when you tell me.'

And it was then I made the decision. I didn't want to go to my lesson. I wanted to get as far away from this place as fast as I could. I turned and ran. David followed for a few yards, calling after me, but then gave up. I didn't care. I didn't care if I never saw him again. With tears in my eyes, I ran blindly out of the main gate.

I ended up in Joe's and sat down in the furthest corner with a cup of coffee and a chocolate biscuit. Now that I'd cooled down, I realised that David was right. I really was behaving in a most irrational manner. And now I'd made matters worse by walking out of school – an act which would promptly be reported to Mr Turnbull.

So. What was I going to do?

Go home? But the headmaster had said he was going to send for my father. Which meant that home was certainly no sanctuary. So where? I wondered.

I looked round the cafe. There were six or seven other fifth form pupils there, playing the fruit machines or listening to the pulsating beat of pop music. They too had been warned; warned about their behaviour; warned about coming to Joe's during lesson time. But despite the threats, they still came. If they could do it, then so could I!

And yet I knew that my punishment would be worse than theirs. I was expected to conform, to behave as the school and my parents expected me to behave. But I was fed up with doing exactly as I was told. I wanted freedom. I wanted to be myself — not what others demanded.

My coffee finished, I rose and walked out of the cafe. I was restless. Every muscle in my body, every part of me, seemed to be tingling, taut with frustration, screaming to be relieved. I walked through the streets, the sun strong in my face, not knowing where I was going, just trying to get rid of the tensions that had built up in me.

Then I saw him. Jago! Filling up his motorcycle with petrol at the service station on the edge of town. I started to run. Sharon's threats were meaningless now. If Jago wanted to take me for a spin on his bike, what business was it of hers? What business was it of anybody's? I was a person. I could do just what I liked. I didn't have to answer to anyone.

Jago turned when I called. 'How come you're not in school?'

I shrugged my shoulders. 'I'd had enough. Thought I'd take the day off.'

He looked at me, disbelieving; curious. 'Honest?'

'Of course honest. I just couldn't take any more.'

Then he laughed. 'Yeah. Know how you feel. Felt like that meself . . . always. What are you planning to do now?'

'I don't know . . . I thought . . . I thought we could go for a spin. Like Sunday. I really enjoyed myself . . . On one condition though.'

'Oh, yeah. What's that?'

'You let me pay for the petrol.'

He looked at me thoughtfully for a moment. 'It's a deal. Has to be – seeing I'm short of the ready.'

The speed at which he snatched the five-pound note from my hand startled me. David would have made all sort of excuses before I forced him to take it. But Jago was different. Jago was Jago. I shouldn't have been surprised.

He put more petrol into the tank. 'Where do you fancy going?'

'I don't mind. Anywhere. Just as long as it's far away from here.'

'Right. Let's think. How about further up the coast? I know of this smashing little place.'

'Suits me,' I said as he kicked the bike into life.

The ride was even better than the one on Sunday. We rode along the main road for about twenty miles. The fresh spring air rushed past, slapping my face, catching my breath and making me gasp. Then Jago turned along the narrow country road of a narrow peninsula that probed its finger into the sea. We banked and swerved past fields and hedges until, coming to the top of a hill, I saw the sea ahead – a sudden flash of blue between land and sky. Then we descended steeply for a hundred yards or so and seconds later pulled into a small village of thatched cottages.

It was midday, and since I hadn't had any breakfast, my stomach was rumbling. And then I discovered to my dismay that I'd left my sandwiches in my locker at school.

'Not to worry,' Jago assured me. 'We'll get something from that shop.' He pointed to one of the cottages which had an ice-cream sign outside.

'But I thought you didn't have any money.'

He grinned and tapped his nose. 'Leave it to me. I'll be back in a couple of minutes.'

He strolled over to the shop and a few minutes later, he was back, a bottle of cider under his arm. He tossed me a pork pie. I caught it and looked at it doubtfully.

'You didn't steal this, did you, Jago?'

'Of course I didn't. What gave you that idea?'

'Jago!' I warned. 'I mean it. I don't like the idea of you stealing.'

He leaned against his bike. 'I'm telling the truth. I bought that all right.' He delved into his leather jacket. 'These are the things I nicked!'

He brought out two pasties, a sausage roll and a packet of chocolate digestive biscuits.

'Oh, Jago. How could you?' That shopkeeper had to pay for those.'

'Come off it. She won't miss a few things like these. Anyhow, I didn't pinch that pork pie. Straight up, I didn't. So you can eat it without troubling your conscience.' He picked up his helmet. 'Come on. Let's get out of this breeze.'

We found a deep hollow in the sand dunes and lay down. Above, spikey clumps of marram grass, clinging to the tops of the dunes, fluttered in the strong breeze.

But down in the hollow, the air wasn't even stirring and the sun was strong.

I still wasn't sure about the pork pie. And told him so. Again.

He convinced me eventually that he hadn't stolen it — or the flagon of cider either. He passed me the bottle and I took a few sips. Bubbles tickled my nose and made me sneeze. I handed it back and wiping the top with the palm of his hand, he tilted it to his lips and took huge gulps until there was less than half the bottle left. Then he took a sausage roll and ate almost all of it in one gigantic bite — like a ravenous dinosaur.

He squinted at me. 'You're funny — you know that?'

'Funny? What do you mean?' I wasn't sure whether to be insulted or not.

'What I say. Funny. I mean, you're so —' he screwed up his eyes as he tried to find the right word, ' — so honest, I suppose. All this palaver about the grub. It won't get you nowhere. If you're hungry, who cares where it comes from?'

'I care. I care because that woman had to pay for it.'

'So what? She can afford it better than I can.'

'That's not the point. What if someone stole something of yours — your gauntlets perhaps — how would you feel about it? Would you like it?'

He shrugged his shoulders. 'I wouldn't — but if someone did pinch me gauntlets, I'd pinch a pair from someone else.'

I gave a cry of sheer exasperation. 'Oh, Jago. You're impossible.'

'Yeah. I know,' he said with a grin. 'But you still like me, don't you?' He held out his hand. 'Give us a lift up and we'll go down to the beach.'

I pulled him to his feet and together we scrambled over the dunes. It was colder on the seashore. The air was fresh and clean and the waves were snowy white as they tumbled and seethed upon the sand.

We ran hand in hand, and once I took off my shoes and paddled in the foam. I felt it sting my legs – and then my toes went numb. Jago didn't join me though; he stood on the edge.

'Get out of there, you idiot!' he shouted. 'Your feet'll fall off.'

He was right, of course, but when I came out, I kicked water into his face. He darted after me as, giggling like a child, I splashed along the edge. Then he caught me. Twisting me round, he held me in his arms. I could feel the brute strength of his body through his thick leather jacket. Our faces were close together, and as I looked up at him the laughing stopped. He held my head in the palm of his hand and kissed me.

He didn't kiss me as David did; soft and gentle. Jago's was harder, more forceful, more demanding. I couldn't move and I couldn't breathe. I pushed hard, desperately trying to twist my head away. Eventually he let me go and there was amusement in his eyes.

'Please . . . please take me home!' I muttered.

He shook his head as though sadly disappointed. 'Sure . . . if that's what you want . . .'

I trembled most of the way home; that kiss had frightened me. And when he dropped me at the end of the street, he asked me round to his place that evening.

'We're having a party,' he explained. 'Just a few of me mates.'

I shook my head. 'Thanks, Jago. But I'd better not. I've got some work to catch up on.'

But my words didn't fool him. 'There's no need to be

scared,' he said quietly. 'I'd never hurt you. I promise. But – ' he swung his bike in a semi-circle ' – if you change your mind . . .'

He drove away and as I watched him go, I felt strangely foolish. I'd had a wonderful time, and felt much better. All my tensions had drained away – and I had no one but Jago to thank for that. Still, I decided, it would be wiser not to accept his invitation. My father would be furious if I went to one of Jago's parties.

I walked back to the house, feeling happy and contented, little realising the reception that awaited me there.

Chapter 14

My father rushed into the hall before I could even close the door. He stood for a moment, framed in the light streaming into the living room.

'Dianne! Thank God you're safe.' As he took a few steps towards me, his shoulders sagged and there was a mixture of despair and relief in his voice. 'I've been worried sick about you. I was about to go to the police.'

I should have realised of course that he would have searched for me as soon as the headmaster contacted him, but I had been so intent upon enjoying my few hours of freedom that I hadn't given him a thought. Suddenly I felt guilty.

'I'm sorry, Dad. I know I should have phoned you, but I was all right – honestly, I was.'

As I took off my coat, he peered at me anxiously. 'But why did you do it? That's what I can't understand. Why did you run out of school like that? It's not like you, Dianne.'

'It's a long story, Dad. Do you think I could have some coffee first?'

He followed me into the kitchen and watched as I filled the kettle. 'But where did you go? I've looked everywhere for you.'

I shrugged my shoulders. 'I just couldn't take any more – school, I mean – I had to get away.'

'But where did you go?' he insisted. 'Things were coming right for once. That's why I phoned the school – to tell you about your mother.'

'Mum? What about Mum?'

'She's coming home tomorrow – for the weekend. I wanted you to get the place ready.'

I felt happiness surge through me. 'Oh, Dad. That's fantastic. It means she's getting well . . . really well, doesn't it?'

He nodded as I brushed past him into the living room. 'But you still haven't told me where you've been.'

I wasn't sure whether to tell him or not. Perhaps it would be better to lie, knowing how he felt about Jago.

'As I said – it's a long story. It started when I had a fight with Sharon Pearson . . .'

That wasn't quite true. It had started when I saw David talking to Stacy, but looking at it coldly, it sounded ridiculous.

'That much I know. What was it over? It's not like you to get into a situation like that.'

I decided to ignore his question. 'Then I was taken to

the headmaster.'

'And he gave you a telling-off. What happened then?'

I was deliberately playing for time, knowing where the questioning was leading. 'I came out and . . . and David was waiting . . .'

'So?'

'Oh, Dad. I'd had enough. Can't you understand how I felt?'

It was now his turn to evade my question. 'Where did you go, Dianne? That's all I want to know.'

I hesitated and then made the decision. 'I went for a ride with Jago,' I said.

There was silence for a few minutes. Then: 'You did what?' The words came hissing out.

'I met Jago – we went for a spin on his bike.'

Dad's face went white; his hands were clenched. 'What did I tell you about that boy? I told you I didn't want you to associate with him.'

'Oh, Dad. He's not as bad as people think.'

'Bad? Not bad?' He shook his head in furious exasperation. 'You know the trouble we've had with him. I've told you.'

I thought of the things he'd stolen from the shop that morning. The knowledge made me feel guilty. And then I was angry with myself.

'He can be very kind,' I muttered, conscious of conflicting emotions.

'Kind? Honestly, Dianne. I can't understand what's happened to you recently. You stick up for a lout like that . . . What would your mother say if she knew you'd been seeing him?'

Suddenly, something snapped inside me. 'And what would she say if she knew that you'd been seeing Liz

Sinclair?'

I could have bitten off my tongue.

He went still. 'I don't know what you mean.'

'Oh, Dad.' I said wearily, my anger now dissipated. 'You know very well what I mean.'

'No, I don't.'

The fact that he was denying it so blatantly made the anger flare again. It burst like a flame inside me. Tears welled up in my eyes.

'Oh why do you deny it? Everyone knows you've been seeing her – and while Mum's in hospital too.'

His face was grave as he turned away. 'It's not what you think.'

I couldn't believe he was saying all this; it just wasn't possible. 'Not what I think, Dad? It's what everybody thinks – Mrs Judd, David, his mother and father. Even Sharon Pearson – why do you think I had that fight with her?'

He sat down heavily, shook his head and sighed. 'I'm sorry, Dianne. I didn't realise . . .'

I left him there and went up to the sanctuary of my room. I felt sorry now. Sorry that I'd been so callous, and I felt a sense of shame overwhelm me. I shouldn't have revealed what I knew.

It was almost an hour later when he called me down to dinner. We ate in silence, neither of us knowing what to say to each other. It was I who broke the ice.

'What time is Mum coming home tomorrow?' I asked as we were eating our sweet.

'About half-past ten. I'm taking her clothes down this evening.'

'Oh, I see . . .'

'She'll stay the night, and then I'll take her back after tea on Sunday.'

132

We were talking like strangers — our conversation stilted and formal. Much too polite after what had occurred.

'Are you going out tonight?' he asked.

I nodded. 'I'll probably call over to see Erica.'

'Good. Don't be home late though. I shan't . . .' I knew what he was doing. In his own way, he was telling me that he wouldn't be seeing Liz. I wondered if he'd ever see her again, now that he was aware that all the neighbours knew.

Erica was surprised to see me. 'Where on earth have you been all day?' she exclaimed, standing aside to let me in. 'Don't you know everybody's been looking for you?'

'I do now.'

'Your father was down at the school — I saw him going into Mr Turnbull's room. Honestly, I've never seen him looking so worried. Anyway, where did you go?'

'I went for a spin with Jago.'

'Jago Brown? After that scrap with Sharon?'

'Because of the scrap with Sharon,' I replied defiantly.

Erica shook her head. 'What's David going to say when he finds out?'

'What can he say? He's got Stacy Heatherington now.'

'Stacy Heatherington?' She looked at me in amazement and laughed aloud. 'But he can't stand her.'

'Huh! I wish I could believe that.'

'But it's true. He told Bob . . . and Bob told me . . .'

'Then why did he have her round to his place last night?'

'Because she more or less forced her way in, that's why. He couldn't get rid of her fast enough.'

I wanted to believe her, but I couldn't forget the scene outside the sixth form common room earlier that day — and the way he had blushed, guilt plainly marking his face.

Abruptly, I changed the subject. 'Do you fancy coming out tonight?' I asked.

'Oh, Dianne. I wish I could. But my parents are going out and I've promised to look after The Brat.'

The Brat was her six-year-old brother, and I knew it to be a term of endearment because though she often complained about him, she really idolised him.

'Why don't you stay here?' she suggested. 'I could phone Bob and David and invite them round.'

I debated whether or not to accept. Then I shook my head. 'No, thanks. Some other time perhaps.' I just didn't feel like meeting David until I'd sorted everything out.

After leaving Erica, I walked around for a while, trying to rid myself of the restlessness that seemed to be deep down in my bones. Finally, I sat on a bench overlooking town. Directly below were the playing fields. The school was on the opposite side, and beyond that the town centre. I could see the sodium street lights on the promenade fringing the sea like an amber ribbon. And further away still was the older part of town — the part where Jago lived — its mean little streets forming a grid, its rigid lines dark and bleak in the gathering dusk. I thought of Jago's invitation — and my father's antagonism towards him.

I was tempted to accept since there was nowhere else to go. However, Sharon would surely be there and another confrontation was something I could well do without. She would now know that Jago and I had spent the whole day together at the seaside.

But threats had always been a challenge. Why should I let anyone – Sharon or my father – prevent me going? This was a free country. I was old enough to do what I liked. I didn't have to have anyone's permission to go to a party. I could do anything I wanted to.

Defiantly, I got to my feet and walked towards town.

I made my way to Jago's house, taking the short cut through the playing fields and crossing the river by the rickety pedestrian bridge. I didn't know exactly where he lived, just that it was somewhere in Sebastapol Street. As I walked apprehensively down the long terrace, I could well believe that the crumbling houses had been built during the Crimean War.

But I need not have worried. I soon found which house was Jago's. The blare of the record player hit me before I was within a hundred yards of it. The thin faded curtains were wide open and I could see Jago standing in the middle of the room, a glass in his hand.

I stood there for a moment, uncertainty once more making me diffident. The small front garden was over-grown with weeds; the gate hung forlornly on one hinge. It was like being in another world – like travelling back a century in time. Here was squalor and the transparent poverty made me cringe.

Then I shook myself. This is ridiculous, I said; just because I came from a home that lacked none of the physical comforts didn't mean I should look down on Jago's. My father had a good job; Jago didn't even have a father. What I felt was sheer snobbery, I had to remind myself.

I walked up the path, which was cracked and

uneven, and pressed a bell that didn't work. There was no knocker; it had long ago disappeared and only a rusted letter flap showed where once it had been. So I hammered on the woodwork and saw the dark green paint flake on to my hand.

The door opened almost at once and Sharon stood there. Instinctively, I took a step backwards.

'Hi, Dianne!' she said, giving me one of her brightest smiles. 'Jago said you might be coming. Why don't you come in and join the fun?'

Chapter 15

Sharon stood aside to let me in. Behind her stood Kenny Chapman, tall and lank, guarding the door against intruders. Jago was now in the kitchen, helping himself to another beer. He waved when he saw me and held up a can of lager. When I nodded, he pulled the ring, and foam gushed down the side.

'Glad you've changed your mind,' he said after he'd squeezed his way past the half-dozen people who thronged the narrow hallway. He handed me the can – no glass – and I took a sip. Foam fizzed up, getting into my nose and making me sneeze.

'This is Dianne,' he yelled above the strident boom of pop music.

Some of them I knew vaguely. Some waved, interest flickering momentarily in their eyes before they forgot about me. One – a guy with a shaven head and a large safety pin through his ear – took no notice; he was shaking his head backwards and forwards in time to the frenetic beat and seemed oblivious of everyone. Then Jago took me into the lounge – if you could call it that – and introduced me to the others. Although measuring roughly twelve feet square, the room was devoid of furniture and the part of the carpet I could see was threadbare, its pattern dulled by years of neglect. The room was packed, a few dancing in the centre while the others sat on the floor, their backs to the wall. All had a can or bottle in their hands; some even had large flagons of beer which they periodically raised to their lips. I didn't think it was possible to get so many people into so small a room.

I felt myself viewing the scene with distaste.

Jago put his arm round my shoulder. 'Glad you came?' he said.

I just about heard him. 'Of course!' I yelled back, knowing there was nothing else I could say. But already, I was beginning to regret my decision.

'I've taken out all the furniture,' he explained as he pushed his way into a corner and sat down. 'All it needs is for some idiot to start walking all over my mother's settee and putting his foot through it . . . You can imagine what the old girl would say.'

Sharon joined us, sat next to Jago and put her arm through his. She smiled across, and again I had an uneasy feeling in the pit of my stomach. It wasn't like her to be so friendly, unless of course she was playing it cool, revealing another side of her character now that Jago was there.

I just couldn't settle down there. I'd never been to a party like it in my life; the noise was deafening and the cigarette smoke, layering the air, made my eyes water. I had two more lagers which made my head spin and an hour later as I was dancing, I knew that coming here had been a mistake. I decided that as soon as it was politely possible, I'd make an excuse and leave.

But then Sharon came up to Jago and whispered something in his ear.

He leaned over. 'Come on,' he said. 'Looks like we've got problems.' He grabbed my hand and hauled me after him into the kitchen where Sharon and Kenny were waiting.

'Now what's all this about running out of booze?'

'Look for yourself.' Kenny nodded at the table behind the door on which were about a dozen cans of beer. 'That lot's not going to last much longer . . .'

Jago ran a hand through his hair. 'Didn't you stand at the door like I told you? Made sure everybody brought something?'

'Of course I did. But I couldn't be in two places at the same time, could I? I couldn't be at the door taking the beer, and in here making sure they didn't drink more than their fair share?'

I became aware that this was a bottle party. 'I'm sorry, Jago. I didn't realise we were expected to bring something.'

'It's all right.' He dismissed my apology with a wave of his hand. 'You haven't drunk much – and besides, you're my guest.' Then he looked pensively at the cans which were left. 'We'll have to get some more . . .that's for certain. Where do you suggest?'

'One of the off-licences?'

Jago was dubious. He glanced at his watch. 'One of the supermarkets would be a better bet.'

I was about to remind him that the supermarkets

were likely to be shut at half-past nine, when Kenny said:

'Reckon we'll need half a dozen cans at least – party size – the way some of these are drinking.'

Jago nodded 'Yeah. Reckon you're right. Which means three or four of us will have to go.'

Sharon spoke for the first time. 'There's four of us here – if you include Dianne. You'll come, won't you?'

There was a look in her eyes that puzzled me. But it was the tone of her voice which annoyed me; it was as though she were challenging me. Which also didn't make sense.

'Of course I'll come,' I replied hotly. 'I'll even put something towards it . . .'

I thrust a hand into my pocket and brought out my purse. For a moment Jago looked suprised; then he began to laugh.

'Put it away, Dianne. We won't be needing that.'

We set out, walking along the back streets, through dark alleyways and narrow footpaths until we came out behind the railway station. Then crossing the line, we clambered over a fence and landed in the lane at the rear of the main shopping street. Jago pulled me sharply into the shadows with the others.

'Right!' he whispered as we gathered round him. 'Which one is it going to be?'

'What about Dianne's father's shop?' It was Sharon who spoke and there was a contemptuous note in her voice. 'After all, she should be able to show us around, shouldn't she?'

Suddenly I knew what they were planning. 'You're not . . . you're not going to break in?' I said, aghast.

Kenny sniggered. 'What you think we've come here

for? A picnic?'

'But you can't . . . you mustn't! Look. I'll give you the money – you can have it all. There's five pounds here.'

I'd spoken too loudly and Jago looked over his shoulder in alarm. 'Keep your voice down, will you? You'll have the fuzz here if you're not careful.'

'But Jago . . . you can't . . .'

He caught hold of my shoulders and shook me. 'I said belt up. Now listen. Use your head, Dianne. You know I can't afford to buy any booze – and your fiver'll buy us hardly nothing!'

'But what if you get caught?' I protested.

'We're not going to get caught,' Sharon hissed, gripping my arm.

They were crowding me now, threatening. I ignored both Sharon and Kenny and addressed Jago.

'But I can't go with you . . . surely you can see that?'

'Why not?'

'Because it's my father's shop. I couldn't do that to him. And anyhow even if it were someone else's . . . Please, Jago! You know I couldn't . . .'

He pondered for a moment. 'All right!' he said at last. 'You'd better get going.'

But Sharon's grip became firmer; her fingers bit into my flesh. 'You can't let her go. What if she tells someone?'

'Yeah. What if she tells someone.' It was Kenny.

'You won't, will you?' Jago's voice sounded gentle in the darkness.

'No . . . I won't . . . I promise . . .'

'Oh, Jago. You're not going to believe her, are you?' Sharon was actually challenging him. 'She'll probably go up to the first cop she sees.'

Jago turned angrily, and when he spoke, his voice was a deep rumble in his throat. 'If she says she won't, she won't. Now let her go.'

Sharon released me, but not before she got the last word in. 'Yes, you're right, Jago. Who wants a girl without guts? We're better off without her.'

I knew then why she had been so welcoming when I arrived. She must have been waiting for an opportunity like this – a chance to show me up in front of Jago. But at that moment, I didn't care what he thought. All I wanted to do was get away.

I ran as fast as I could, across the square and down the avenue that led to the school, not stopping until I arrived at the foot of the hill where the road rose sharply upwards. By that time I was breathing so hard that the cold night air tore at my lungs. My legs felt as heavy as lead. Wearily, I sat on a bench and closed my eyes. What had I almost let myself in for? I asked myself. Why had I been so stupid? Even the most innocent girl would have realised what they had planned – long before they set out from the house. The signs had been there for me to see. Had I deliberately chosen to ignore them?

I thought of my father. Had I been foolish enough to be involved in the break-in – and been caught – then it could well have cost him his job.

But it hadn't happened, I kept telling myself. I hadn't been involved. As soon as I'd realised what they were about to do, I'd left. So why was I worrying? Why was my whole body trembling so much?

I pulled myself to my feet and trudged up the hill, back to the safety of my own home. My father's car wasn't in the drive and yet when I walked into the living room I discovered that the television was still on.

A half-eaten sandwich lay on the table and by its side a cup of coffee. It was still warm. My father could not possibly have been out of the house long, and when he'd left he had obviously been in a hurry.

But where, I wondered, had he gone? Had there been an urgent phone call from the hospital? But I realised almost at once that it wasn't feasible. My mother was in no danger. So why should they have phoned him?

Unless . . . I thought of Jago and the possibility that he might have been caught. My stomach flipped over and I had to shut my eyes tight and hold on to the chair before it righted itself. It was more than a possibility; it was a probability. There was after all an alarm system at the supermarket, wired up to the local police station; but surely Jago would have realised that.

Except that the alarm didn't sound in the shop – which would have lulled them all into a sense of false security.

My mind whirled. There were so many questions – but no answers.

I didn't hear my father's car pull up outside. The first indication I had that he'd returned was the soft metallic click of his key in the lock. Then he appeared at the living-room door.

'So you're home.' He looked completely worn out. Weariness dulled his eyes and his hair seemed even greyer than ever, matching the pallor of his face. 'Thank God for that.'

He flung his coat on a chair, slumped on to the settee, and rubbed his face with his hands.

'Is everything all right?' I asked, my voice sounding tight and strange.

He gave a deep sigh. 'It is now . . .' He shook his head slowly from side to side. 'But I can tell you, when I got that telephone call . . .'

'Telephone call?'

'From the police. Someone had broken into the supermarket. Two boys and a girl they told me. I thought . . .' He stood up, crossed to the cocktail cabinet, and poured himself a large scotch. '. . . But I was wrong . . . thank God I was wrong . . .'

He returned to the settee, leaned back, his legs stretched out in front of him.

'It was Jago Brown and a couple of his friends — caught red-handed.' He looked at me for a moment, took a sip of his whisky, and then said slowly:

'Thank God you had the sense to keep away from him tonight!'

Chapter 16

This time I couldn't tell him the truth. Not only because he looked so weary, but also for the fact that telling him would have served no useful purpose. After all, I hadn't been with Jago and the others when they'd broken in. The moment their intentions became apparent, I had done my best to dissuade them. And when that had failed, I'd left. Telling my father would only have caused him worry.

Besides, I kept telling myself, I was in the clear. No one could connect me with their crime.

I stood up. 'Would you like a coffee? I'm going to take one up to bed.'

'Why not?' He held up his glass, measuring the contents. 'And I think I'll have another one of these too.'

While I prepared the coffee, I heard him pour another scotch, and a few minutes later, as I carried in the mugs, he was seated in his chair, frowning thoughtfully into the fire.

'Before you go up, Dianne,' he said as I handed him the mug, 'there's something I'd like to talk to you about.'

Intuitively, I knew what it was. 'There really is no need,' I said huskily.

'But there is,' he insisted. He couldn't help being aware of my reluctance. 'Please, Dianne. Sit down. Just for a few minutes. It won't take long.'

I sat opposite him and waited. For a few seconds he said nothing and it was obvious that he was choosing his words carefully.

'Look. About your mother and me.' He paused and breathed in deeply. 'Things haven't been good between us for some time, but I don't suppose I have to tell you that. Though I think you ought to know that we tried hard not to quarrel when you were around . . . we tried to hide it from you . . .'

'That was stupid!' I muttered. 'How could you possibly hope to do that?'

'I know – but we tried – neither of us wanted to involve you. Anyway, it got so bad in the end we could barely exchange a few words without it developing into a full-blown quarrel. In the end, I actually dreaded coming home. And I think if it hadn't been for you, I would have walked out ages ago.' He sighed again, leaned forward, his elbows resting on his knees, staring at the floor. Out in the bay, a ship's siren hooted mournfully.

'I'm not saying it was all your mother's fault. Probably none of it was. She was ill, and I should have been more understanding – more sympathetic– but it wasn't easy. Then a few months ago, Liz – Liz Sinclair – came to work at the supermarket and we became friendly.'

He paused and looked straight at me. 'I don't expect you to understand, Dianne. Not at your age. And believe me, I'm not making any excuses for my behaviour. But for the first time in months – years perhaps – I felt free from pressure. Just to have someone to talk to . . . to be able to laugh again . . . I don't know. It's difficult to explain.'

He didn't expect me to understand? I understood far more than he suspected. I understood only too well what it was like to be under pressure. I knew the urgent desire to get away from it all. That's why I'd been attracted to Jago. That's why I'd found his company so refreshing.

'Anyway,' he went on, 'it's all over now. I shan't be meeting Liz again . . . apart from work of course. All I can do now is hope that your mother won't find out.'

Without saying it in so many words, he was asking – begging – me not to divulge his secret to my mother.

'But what if she does find out? What if someone tells her? One of the neighbours perhaps?'

He nodded thoughtfully. 'You're right, of course. That's a distinct possibility . . . and really I should confess. But not now. Not when she's ill. Later, when she's strong enough, I probably will. And beg her forgiveness.'

He glanced at his watch and stood up. 'It's late, Dianne. We've both got a lot to do tomorrow. I think it's time we went to bed.'

I walked to the door and turned round. 'If it's any consolation, Dad,' I said, 'I won't tell Mum anything. I wouldn't want to hurt her, would I?'

He smiled sadly. 'No, I'm sure you wouldn't. I don't think either of us would.'

I lay awake for hours, unable to sleep because of the thoughts that jarred upon my mind. I was like my father in so many ways, and like my father I had behaved foolishly over the past weeks – with results that could have been disastrous. Every time I thought of that dark lane behind the supermarket with the wind whipping along it, my stomach began to churn. If I hadn't had the courage to break away, then I too would have been caught. My mother would have known and I dreaded to think what effect that would have had upon her.

And upon my father too!

I thought of the headlines in the local press: 'Daughter Breaks Into Father's Supermarket.' The publicity would have cost him his job.

I thrust the image from my mind. It wasn't worth thinking about. I had learned my lesson. I wouldn't be seeing Jago again – just as my father wouldn't be meeting Liz Sinclair.

I was sorry now that I'd challenged my father about his relationship with her. I could still remember the shame in his eyes and the pain that followed it. Yet at the same time, I was glad. Not only had I been relieved of the frustration of knowing and not being able to do a thing about it, but I had learned something about my father.

He wasn't the infallible person I'd idolised as a child — strong, supportive, always around when needed. He had his weaknesses too, and strangely I loved him all the more because of them.

I thought of David. And Jago. David so reliable and hardworking, and Jago so carefree and exciting. Yet I knew deep down that David would prove the best friend in need, even though he barely had time to breathe now that his examinations were so near.

Poor Jago! He wasn't vindictive — not like Sharon who wouldn't have hesitated to get me into trouble if it suited her purpose; Jago was just wild and reckless.

But the thought of Sharon made me sit up in bed and switch on my table lamp.

She was vindictive enough to tell the police that I'd been with them. That I'd been a look-out perhaps who'd managed to get away. I recalled the way she had cried in front of Miss Paige, declaring her innocence. It would be something she'd do without the slightest hint of remorse. My mind raced with the possibilities.

Or perhaps they might suspect that I'd informed the police and that was why they'd been caught. In which case I could surely expect reprisals of some kind — from Sharon if not from Jago. I slumped back on my pillow and closed my eyes. So I wasn't out of trouble yet.

It was after I heard the distant chimes of the town church strike out the hour of two that eventually I dozed off into a sleep plagued with dreams.

I was back at the supermarket, with Sharon dragging me through the rear entrance. She was jeering, maliciously forcing me to the very front of the store, insisting that I took cans of lager from the window display itself. I was aware, even in my dream, that I was likely to be caught. Then Sharon wasn't with me. I was alone. I looked up and there on the other side of the plate-glass window was my father, pointing an accusing finger at me. I stared in horror, and in front of my eyes, he changed. He seemed to dissolve, melting into waving lines, and then became transformed into a policeman.

I turned and raced down a never-ending avenue of shelves. At the far end were Jago and Sharon. They were urging me to hurry. But the faster I ran, the further away they seemed to get. My legs seemed to drag, and as I glanced desperately over my shoulder, I saw hordes of men in dark blue uniforms jostling in pursuit.

I reached the door only to have it slam in my face. Sharon was on the other side, laughing in derision. But just as I was about to be caught, I found myself in the middle of the square, alone and terrified, with policemen surging in all directions. Then began a frantic chase through town, down wide streets and narrow lanes, across patches of waste ground strewn with rubbish and over barren open fields.

And all the time I was being pursued by a swelling mass of men.

I arrived at the natural platform in the hillside above town where Jago had once taken me. But now, instead of a gentle slope, there was a precipice. Below – far far below – thunderous waves crashed on to jagged rocks. I turned to find myself ringed by a semi-circle of police officers. The sight made me recoil in horror. For not one of them had a face. They were standing still – silent yet menacing. Then, as though at a given signal, they moved nearer, one step at a time, closing the gap between us. I shuffled fearfully backwards until my heels were touching the edge. I glanced over my shoulder. The waves were raging, dashing themselves in a fury against the rocks. They seemed to be alive, seething torrents of foam that exploded upwards.

One of the men stepped forward, and as he did so, his face took form. It became my father's face, stern and forbidding. He stretched out a hand. I jerked away and lost my balance. I felt myself totter; my arms flailed in the air as my whole body strove to regain a foothold. Then I was falling, tumbling through the air, the world spinning around me, a kaleidoscope of earth and sky and sea. I actually heard myself scream.

I awoke in a cold sweat to find myself in my father's arms and sobbing like a child. 'It's all right.' His voice was soothing. 'You've just had a nightmare. That's all.'

Gradually, I composed myself, wiping my eyes on the sleeve of my nightdress and feeling foolish. I looked up and saw my father grinning. 'You scared me when you started screaming,' he said. 'I thought someone was trying to murder you.' Then he stood up. 'I'll get you a coffee. That'll make you feel better.'

He returned almost immediately. 'Better not stay in bed too long,' he said. 'We've got a lot to do this morning.'

It took twenty minutes for the trembling to stop and by that time I'd decided exactly what I had to do. To sit around and worry, waiting for trouble, was futile. I was going to meet it head on. I was going to see Jago himself.

It was obvious when I got downstairs that Dad had been up early. Every room had been vacuumed, the furniture had been dusted and polished, and the living-room windows had been cleaned. The bright morning sunshine made the whole room gleam and the smell of lavender polish bestowed upon the place a fresh country atmosphere.

I refused breakfast, deciding even against toast and helped myself instead to another cup of coffee. As we sat opposite each other, my father looked across.

'I'll be leaving soon to collect your mother. Do you think you could do the washing up as well as get lunch ready? I think I've done everything else.'

'Of course.' Now that I'd decided what to do, I felt much better. 'What's for lunch anyway?'

'I thought a salad . . . and perhaps some fruit and ice cream for dessert.'

I agreed. Mum usually enjoyed a salad even in the middle of winter, and though I hadn't yet ventured into the garden, I knew that the breeze that stirred the budding cherry tree was warm and gentle. Besides, it was simple to prepare – which would give me plenty of time to get round to Jago's. A task I wasn't looking forward to with much enthusiasm.

'Oh, yes. And perhaps you could tidy your room. I have a suspicion that the first thing your mother will want to do is prowl around the house to make sure everything is in order.'

I smiled at him, feeling my confidence return with every minute that passed. 'Of course I will. It won't take me long.'

At that moment, the front door bell rang. My father went to answer it, leaving the doors wide open as he went. I heard him slide back the bolts and a second or two later the front door opened.

'Mind if I see Dianne a minute, mister?' said a voice.

My heart almost stopped beating. It was Jago.

He had obviously come to make trouble. Now my father would discover where I was last night.

Chapter 17

I found my father standing in the doorway, legs astride, blocking the way. 'No, you damn well can't. You can clear off!'

'Look, mister. I'm not here to make trouble.' He had taken off his crash helmet and his dark hair was plastered to his forehead. 'I just want to talk to her, that's all.'

My father stepped outside, pushing Jago backwards with the palm of his hand. 'Don't you "mister" me. I said clear off . . . and I mean clear off!'

I'd never seen Dad so aggressive. I hurried down the hall and caught his arm. 'No, Dad. Let him say what he has to. Please . . .'

He might as well get it over with, I thought; though it was a pity my father had to know.

Dad looked at me, then at Jago, then back at me again. 'All right,' he said at last. 'But not out here. You'd better come in.'

He stood aside, let Jago past, and shut the door. 'That's as far as you're coming into this house,' he said, pointing to the floor. 'Now have your say and go.'

'Dad! Please!' I said, embarrassed at the way he was treating him. 'Don't be like that.'

Jago's eyes flickered towards me and then at my father. 'I just came to tell you I'm sorry – both of you –' he glanced warily at my father ' – for breaking into the shop last night. I shouldn't have done it, I know – especially since I know you, Dianne. Anyway, I'm sorry. That's what I came to say, mister.'

I don't know which of us was the more surprised: me or my father.

For Jago to apologise to anyone was completely out of character and for a few seconds, we looked at him, totally perplexed. Then, getting no reply, Jago turned and went to the door.

'Hey! Hold on!' My father suddenly came alive.

Jago paused, his hand on the door handle. 'What is it, mister?'

'You didn't come here this morning hoping we wouldn't prosecute, did you?' The thought had also occurred to me. 'Because if you did,' he warned, 'it won't do you any good. The matter's in the hands of the police.'

Contempt glinted in Jago's eyes. 'Come off it, mister. Try to get myself off the hook? The police have been waiting for something like this for ages.' He shook his head. 'No, mister. Like I said; I only came here to say I was sorry.'

He lumbered down the path, leaving my father looking decidedly awkward. Though I knew my father wouldn't approve, I hurried after Jago.

'He doesn't believe me, does he?' he muttered angrily. 'Just because I'm always in trouble, doesn't mean I don't tell the truth . . . sometimes . . .'

'I think he does now, Jago.'

He mounted his motorcycle and looked at me. He grinned. 'Yeah. Perhaps you're right. He doesn't know you were with us last night though, does he?'

'No he doesn't – and thanks for not telling him.' I paused, summoning up the courage to speak. 'About last night – you know it wasn't me, don't you? I didn't tell the police.'

'Of course I know. I told the others you wouldn't grass on us – you're not that kind of girl, even though it was your father's shop.'

'I bet Sharon didn't think so.'

He scratched his nose. 'She does now. She wanted to tell the fuzz about you, but I told her: no way – we don't tell the fuzz nothing. And I told her to leave you well alone.'

So he did know about the fight we'd had. I breathed a sigh of relief. Not only wouldn't I be involved with the police, but Sharon wouldn't come seeking vengeance again. Jago had spoken!

'What will they do? The police, I mean.'

'I don't know. They'll probably put me down. That's what they said would happen if I appeared before the beak again.'

I gasped in dismay. 'Oh, no. Don't say that.'

'Who cares? It won't be that bad. Three good meals a day – a roof over my head – plenty of mates . . .'

He was putting on a show of bravado, but if he thought he was fooling me, he was wrong. He turned his head away and putting on his helmet, pulled down the visor abruptly.

'One other thing.' His voice was thick and I didn't think it was merely the scarf he was winding round his lower jaw that muffled it. 'I think it's best if you don't bother with us any more – for your own good. You're not like us, Dianne; you're different. You proved that last night. If it had been my old man's shop, I wouldn't have thought twice about breaking in – only I'd have made sure I knew where the alarm points were. Wouldn't have got caught then, would I?'

He kicked his motorcycle into life. 'See you around!' he yelled with a wave of his hand. Then, revving up the engine, he pulled away with a roar and left the air reeking with the pungent smell of burning rubber.

I felt sad. He had been right when he'd told me to stay away. I was different, though like Jago I too was a prisoner. My life had been planned for me by parents who thought more of me than they did of themselves. I had friends who would stand by me, and a whole future opening up ahead of me. In spite of everything, my life was better than his.

Jago had nothing. Just his wits – and a lifetime of trouble. And yet there was something good there. All too briefly I had seen it.

I returned to my father. His eyes sought anxiously for any sign I might give.

'It's all right! ' I assured him. 'I won't be seeing him again.'

He gave a deep sigh. 'Thank God for that. He's no good – you do realise that, don't you? Not to you or anyone else. Not even to himself. He'd only have caused you a great deal of unhappiness.'

I nodded and bit my lip, knowing too that Jago wouldn't have hurt me deliberately. Yet even so, through my association with him, I had come close – so close – to calamity.

I gave my father a smile that hid my true feelings. 'Perhaps I'd better get lunch ready. Do you think Mum would like a baked potato with her salad?'

About ten minutes after my father drove away, the bell rang a second time. Wondering who it could be, I opened the door to discover David standing outside.

His face was solemn; almost grim. 'Hi.' He glanced over my shoulder at the open door which led into the lounge. 'Is your father in? I'd like to speak to you – alone, if that's possible . . .'

My stomach went tight. 'Yes, yes of course – I was about to make some coffee. Would you like some?'

'That would be great.' He said it without enthusiasm. Then he followed me down the hall and standing at the door, watched me fill the kettle. This wasn't the usual David. He was behaving like a stranger – like someone who had some unpleasant news to impart. 'I came along to tell you . . .'

Tell me what? I remembered what Erica had said the previous night. She had tried to be kind when she assured me that David didn't even like Stacy. She had tried to protect me by staving off the inevitable. But the inevitable had arrived.

'. . . I wanted to tell you I'm sorry for the way I behaved towards you yesterday.'

Now he was trying to soften the blow.

'It's all right.'

'But it isn't all right. I shouldn't have said what I did.'

'You were right. I needed to cool down.'

'That didn't give me the authority to order you around . . .' He hesitated and suddenly there was a glimmer of uncertainty in his eyes. 'But that's not what I wanted to speak to you about.'

I handed him his coffee and he followed me into the living room. 'I wanted to explain about Stacy.'

This was it, I thought. Tears welled up in my eyes. 'It's all right,' I muttered huskily. 'I realise she's much prettier than me.'

There was a moment's silence, and then:

'What on earth are you talking about?' He almost exploded, and there was a note of incredulity in his voice. 'She's not prettier than you.'

I looked up in surprise. 'You don't think so?'

'Of course I don't! And even if it were true, it wouldn't make any difference. I can't stand the girl. That coy little girl act she puts on gives me the creeps.'

'But why did you come?'

He ran a hand through his fair hair. 'Come off it, Dianne. I came to ask you out tonight . . . to the disco . . . anywhere . . . Well? What do you say?'

There was a lump in my throat. 'Oh, David. You know I will.'

By the time he left about half an hour later we had arranged to meet at eight that evening, and as he walked jauntily down the road, I couldn't help smiling. And kicking myself for ever having doubted him.

I went upstairs and began to get my room ship-shape in time for Mum's return. For a moment or two, I gazed out at a sea that shimmered and sparkled in the bright spring sunshine.

So much had happened in the past few weeks. I had caused myself and others – my father in particular – so much trouble. I'd neglected my work, annoyed my friends, and almost landed myself in serious trouble. But that was all over now. I couldn't run away from my problems; I had to face up to them. Conquer them. Just as I had to pass my 'O' levels.

Though I'd wasted almost six weeks, I had two things in my favour. I had worked hard until the middle of the term; if I worked hard from now on, I'd soon catch up. And with my mother improving . . .

The thought of my mother made me realise that soon she would be arriving. I glanced at the clock on my bedside cabinet. Dad had been gone more than an hour. Assuming it took half an hour to get to the hospital, a few minutes while he went to the ward, and another half hour for the return journey, he should be home soon.

It was time to put on the kettle for the cup of tea to which my mother was so addicted. I hurried downstairs and put out the cups and saucers on a tray together with a plate of her favourite biscuits. Then, after a quick examination of all the rooms to see that everything was in order, I returned upstairs to change.

I wondered what to wear. I hated dresses, particularly when I was just lounging around the house, but my mother liked to see me in one – particularly the one she'd bought me for Christmas. Just to please her, I put it on.

I heard my father's car pull into the drive – heard his key turning in the lock – and heard his familiar call as he announced that they were both home.

With my heart fluttering with excitement, I rushed to the top of the stairs. My mother was in the hall and my father was helping her out of her warm red outdoor coat. I couldn't believe my eyes; she looked so different. She was dressed in a black velvet suit and white tie-neck blouse. Her hair had been set, she'd put on weight, she looked healthier – and much much younger. In fact she looked a completely different person.

But the real change was in her eyes. The desperate haunted look had gone and in its place there was a light that made them sparkle. She was the mother I once knew – not so very long ago.

She looked up at me and smiled. 'Hello, darling!' she said and held out her arms.

I gulped as I walked down the stairs. Tears welled up in my eyes, blurring my vision. 'Welcome – welcome home, Mum,' I said in reply, the words sticking in my throat as I took her hands in mine.

Then she pulled me towards her and held me tight. Tears were now streaming down my cheeks as I hugged her. I felt them trickle uncontrollably to my lips; felt their saltiness in my mouth.

But those tears were tears of joy as I basked in the warmth of her embrace. Then my father's arms were around us too, clasping us to him, girding us with his strength.

I knew suddenly with a certainty that defied explanation – standing in the coolness of the hall, laughing and crying at the same time – that the future would be different. For all of us.